THE COLLECTED OLD CURMUDGEON

*Almost Ten Years of Sometimes Enlightening,
Sometimes Just Grumpy Essays from
Price Hill's Most Prolific Grouch*

Roy Hotchkiss

Published by Edgecliff Press, LLC.,
in partnership with the
Price Hill Historical Society
Cincinnati, Ohio

www.edgecliffpress.com

www.pricehill.org

The Collected Old Curmudgeon:
Almost Ten Years of Sometimes Enlightening,
Sometimes Just Grumpy Essays from Price Hill's Most Prolific Grouch

By Roy Hotchkiss

Published by Edgecliff Press, LLC.,

In partnership with the Price Hill Historical Society
Cincinnati, Ohio

www.edgecliffpress.com
www.pricehill.org

ISBN Number 978-0-9819271-1-4

Library of Congress Control Number: 2009932746
Copyright © 2009 by Roy Hotchkiss

10   9   8   7   6   5   4   3   2   1

Published in the United States of America

CONTENTS

Introduction

The Old Curmudgeon's Corner first appeared in the pages of the Price Hill Historical Society's newsletter, *Heritage on the Hill*, in December 1999. It's been a popular feature of the newsletter ever since, and it will certainly continue to grace the pages of the Historical Society newsletter in the future, as long as Roy has something to sound off about. But with more than a hundred Curmudgeon columns already published, we thought it was time for a collection. Heck, Jim Borgman publishes a collection of cartoons just about every year. Speaking of which, the original illustrations by the

By Roy Hotchkiss

Old Curmudgeon himself, Roy Hotchkiss, that appeared with some Curmudgeon columns are also included in this collection. There are also a few new illustrations, as well as some curmudgeonly "Pithy Mots" that Roy has added as an extra bonus for fans of the column. Never before in print! See them here first!

But back to the essays themselves. There are 115 of them, from the first published column in November 1999 to the Society's 19th anniversary column in June 2009 that ends this collection. We thought that would be a good place to stop—celebrating almost twenty years of the Price Hill Historical Society, and almost ten years of the Curmudgeon.

You never know what the Old Curmudgeon might gripe about next—it could be local elections, it could be childproof medicine caps, the holiday season, or just about anything else. Sometimes he takes a month off from griping to answer letters or enlighten us on the origins of some everyday or arcane object or practice. (And for some reason he just didn't write a column in November 2000.) There's never a dull moment with the Old Curmudgeon in the house.

So sit back and enjoy browsing through almost ten years of sometimes enlightening, sometimes just grumpy musings from the Old Curmudgeon.

June 2009
Price Hill, Ohio

DISCLAIMER

Artwork, layout and opinions are preserved as provided by the Hotchkiss' and Price Hill Historical Society. Please note, the oft overworked newsletter editor often did not have the time or energy to check facts at the time of original printing; she was just grateful that someone else had written the actual columns.

The Old Curmudgeon's Corner is an opinion column, and the opinions expressed herein do not necessarily reflect those of the Price Hill Historical Society, its members, Price Hillians, non-Price Hillians, Historians, Librarians, Professional Sports, the Automotive Industry, the Plastics Industry, Packaging Designers, Urban Planners, Construction Workers, Medical Practitioners, Pharmacists, Pharamceutical Companies, MediCare and MedicAid, Television, Film and Radio Industries, Chefs, Bakers' Guilds, Retailers, Carpenters, Organized Religions, Federal, Local and State Governments, Law Enforcement Officials, Computer Users, the Living, the Deceased, Fast Food Chains, Past and Current U.S. Presidents or Tom Robbins.

Reprinting of these essays by Edgecliff Press in partnership with the Price Hill Historical Society is part of an ongoing effort to capture, retain and present Cincinnati history. Likewise, the opinions expressed do not necessarily reflect those of Edgecliff Press, LLC. although we do think Roy is a funny guy.

Enjoy!

Introducing "The Old Curmudgeon's Corner"

November 1999

Curmudgeon, *ker-muj 'on*, n. an irascible, cantankerous person

My grey beard, the appalling diminishing hair on my head, and the crick in my neck certainly qualify me for the "old" part of the title of this piece, and according to the definition above and my wife and daughters, the second part applies as well. So that's what I am calling this column. It may appear regularly or just every once in a while, depending on space available and on whether or not I have something to gripe about.

This month I do have a few items to get off my chest, but I have already taken up a lot of space so I will just offer a couple of complaints.

1. The Cincinnati Recreation Department . . . They couldn't, or wouldn't come up with a feasible way for us to use the building at Carson Covedale Park . . . When they acquired the Allen House property they actually offered this Society the old school building, which would have been great, but almost as soon as the offer was made, they reneged, offering instead an old house up there that needs a lot of repair and doesn't meet our requirements. They want a high rent for it but they can't decide what the rent should be. Our dealings with the CRD have been frustrating to say the least.

2. The Parade . . . The parade will end this year at St. Lawrence Church. I don't have anything to do with the Thanksgiving Day Parade (that's another story), but I thought one of the purposes of it was to draw East and West Price Hill closer together. East Price Hill just got cut out completely. So much for togetherness.

Ye Old Standard Disclaimer: **The Old Curmudgeon** *is an editorial column, and the opinions expressed in it do not necessarily reflect those of the Price Hill Historical Society or its membership.*

REFLECTIONS ON ELECTIONS

December 1999

The elections that took place early last month disturbed me a little. Not so much who got elected, but the small number of voters who elected them. Only 33% of the people in our city voted. That's only 3 people out of 10, and that's only counting registered voters, who elected the men and women who will govern our city for the next two years.

"Well, that's in the whole city," we West-Siders might say. "The people in Hyde Park probably didn't vote at all."

Sorry, but us upstanding Price Hillians didn't do a bit better than the rest of the city. Only about 3 out of 10 voted in our community, too.

We all complain about our "do-nothing" city council, but most of them seem to get back in, year after year. Can the 33% of us that vote only remember the names we hear over and over? If the other 67% got off their duffs, we might get some significant changes.

I have heard people say that their vote wouldn't make any difference. They are right, it won't make any difference if they don't cast it.

Finally, the Thanksgiving Day Parade. I'm writing this before the parade so I don't know how it went off. I talked to several people from East Price Hill who were trying to cook up some kind of a demonstration. I was with them and willing to help, but as far as I know nothing really got planned. Several East Price Hill organizations will not participate, but that seems to be the extent of the protest.

PITHY MOT

What's in a name? Well, names ending in a vowel are apparently very important. Actually, the "best" names end in E, I, or that near-vowel, Y. For some reason, A and U don't work as well, but an O occasionally does the trick. And they were probably more important in past times than today. When I was a kid, if a mother wanted her child to come home, she went out on the back porch and shouted: "Billy!" "Johnnie!" "Toni!" The euphonious vibrations echoed through the neighborhood until they reached the sought-after child and he or she rushed home. Mothers calling "Marvin, Marvin!" or "Algernon!" did not have the same zip or verve, and their plaintive calls often went unanswered.

ANOTHER DARN NEW YEAR

January 2000

Tis the season to be jolly, so I'll be jolly. The latter part of December is a festive time for people of most theologies. Some of us jubilate the conservation of oil, some rejoice at the return of the sun, and others celebrate a birth that took place approximately two millennia ago. Whatever your reason, I wish you the joy of the season.

But speaking of millennia, how sure are we that this next year is really 2000? Let's look into that.

The abbreviation A.D. stands for *Anno Domini*, in the year of our Lord. So 1 A.D. was supposed to be the year of the birth of Jesus Christ, but somebody goofed. Christ was probably born around 6 B.C. The New Testament states that King Herod died in 4 B.C., and he was the ruler of Judea when Christ was born, so it had to be *before* 4 B.C., in any event.

So, who screwed up? If we have to blame somebody, I guess it would be a little-known monk named Dennis. In Dennis's time there was a terrible controversy over Easter. A veritable theomachy arose over the date of the feast of Easter.

Dennis's ambition was to settle this Easter problem once and for all. In the process, he invented a new calendar that began from the birth of Christ. He worked on the math for months, but unfortunately he misplaced a prime number or something, and missed the actual birth date by a few years.

A hundred years later, at the Synod of Whitby in 664, the Church adopted Dennis's calendar. The calendar had more errors in it than just its starting date, but major corrections were not made until Pope Gregory XII got hold of it.

As any good politician would do, Gregory appointed a commission to straighten it out. This commission actually worked at making the proper adjustments, and in 1582 they came up with pretty much the calendar that is in almost universal use today. It is called the Gregorian system, but unfortunately it is still a few years off from the actual birth of Christ.

All the nations of the world are bound together and must have a common ground for marking time, and the Gregorian calendar is generally accepted. However, some other cultures still maintain their own methods of tracking the date. So what year is it anyway?

Einstein said it, "Time is relative." Anyway, "Happy Whatever!"

Visiting the Neighbors

February 2000

I thought our January meeting at the Delhi Historical Society's headquarters was very nice. I enjoyed seeing their building; they have put a lot of work in it and it is beautiful. The outside just sparkles and the inside is almost perfect. Not too much, but everything they have is interesting, historical, and well taken care of. My visit to the farmhouse was most enjoyable and because members of Delhi's society were there to tell us about the house and what their group were planning for the future, I found that night especially gratifying.

If you haven't had a chance to see the Delhi Society's house, you should try to make an effort to go see it. It's the kind of place I hope our group can have some day.

The evening was very rewarding in another way. A few of the Delhi society people and some of us got together and talked about cooperating on some future projects. I think this is a great idea. We are already planning four joint ventures. In May, the Delhi Historical Society and the Price Hill Historical Society are sponsoring an old-time baseball game. It will feature an old-fashioned baseball team called the Muffins playing a "makeup" group of players, in old style uniforms, from around here. They will play following the rules that were used in the late 1800s.

The annual Croquet Match and Horseshoe Pitch between the Delhi and Price Hill historical societies are two other events we've tried before, and we will try to make them more spectacular than they have been in the past. Finally, we will be working on a very special home tour of some houses that are historically significant, not necessarily in either of our areas.

I'm sure I have used up more space than I should so I had better quit before our editor gets after me. But once again, let me say thanks to the Delhi folks.

PITHY MOT

Do you remember when a gas station was a place to get the tank filled, have the windows cleaned, and drain the kids?

Now you have to fill your own tank, clean your own windows, and the only thing that gets drained is your wallet.

GIVE 'EM CIRCUSES

March 2000

I see by the *Enquirer* that the cost of the new stadium is going to be a little higher than we were led to believe. A lot of millions of dollars more!

We, the taxpayers of Hamilton County, were certainly sold a bill of goods on this one. I hope you'll keep in mind exactly who it was that sold us this bill of goods when you make your electoral decision during the upcoming county commissioner race.

The horrendous cost of the stadium is only one of the things bothering me. Apparently it is a wonderful thing that this Mr. Graaff is coming to Cincinnati to play the baseball. I understand that he took a cut in salary just so he could play for the Reds. He turned down thirteen and a half million a year and now will only make a little over twelve million annually. When you make that much do you really miss a million or two?

The salaries of professional athletes have become astronomical, as have those of the performers on television and in the movies. It's unbelievable, all that money just to keep us entertained.

What was it the old Roman senators said before their civilization fell apart? *Donate eis circenses.* Loosely translated, that means "Give 'em circuses." Is that what we are being provided, circuses, so we won't notice when things go awry?

⌘ ⌘ ⌘ ⌘ ⌘ ⌘ ⌘

A friend of many in Price Hill, Franny Lang, passed away this past January. He was 94 years old and a true Price Hillian. He had been very active in the Price Hill Civic Club and was the King of Price Hill in 1998. More importantly, he was a jolly and friendly fellow. I have seen him every couple of weeks for the past several years and he was always bright and outgoing. I talked to him the Sunday before he died and he still had a smile and positive outlook on the world. I'll miss Franny, and I'm sure many other people in Price Hill will miss him too.

A Few Foolish Plans

April 2000

There's big real estate news in Price Hill this month. The Sieve Pontiac property on Ferguson Road has been purchased by a Northern Kentucky religious group. They have scrapped their plans to build a creationist museum in Kentucky and will now utilize the Sieve property to display their exhibits.

The Seminary Square folks are very happy because they are about to get a new seminary in the area. Another religious group, the Reformed Druids, has purchased the park property at Considine and Glenway. They are already planting oak trees around the perimeter of the property. The facility will be circular in design and constructed of large stones.

The Cincinnati Recreation Department soon will raze the old farmhouse at the Carson-Covedale Park on Rapid Run. They had planned to extend their soccer fields, but in the spirit of cooperation they have long shown us, they now plan to put in a fully lighted croquet court.

Finally, the Covedale Theater will not become a teen dance club. The city has purchased the property. They plan to replace the roof with a huge glass dome and landscape the interior with tropical plants and trees and a thirty-foot waterfall. This horticultural wonder will rival the east side's Krohn Conservatory. Mary Bazeley has already requested NSP funds for 40 tons of mulch.

Editor's Note: This **Old Curmudgeon** *column was published on April 1, 2000. Enough said.*

THE SAD STATE OF THE FUNNY PAPERS

May 2000

The new century began April 10. That's what the half-page ads in our local newspapers heralded recently. These are what are called "teaser" ads. I thought they were rather ineffective, since I had no idea what they were teasing about. And personally, I could have cared less.

Apparently, the ads were to prepare us for the changes in format of our two local papers. Technically they were changing the web size of their presses from 54 inches to 50 inches. What that meant to us was that the papers were going to be narrower.

That didn't sound too bad to me, a little less paper, a few trees saved. But I was concerned that the smaller paper would have smaller type. As you get older, the newspaper gets harder and harder to read. I talked to someone at the *Enquirer* and was told not to worry. The old type was about 9.7 points and the redesigned type would be about 9.5 points. That didn't sound so bad. Unfortunately, I wasn't told that the type would also be condensed, or smushed sideways.

The newly designed newspapers did come out on April 10. I found the copy a little harder to read, but I struggled along. There are a lot more colored pictures in these new papers. Sadly, they were almost all out of registration and fuzzy. There were a lot of smudges, which made my perusal even more difficult. Then I came to the comic section.

I am an avid follower of the comic strips. One of my earliest recollections is reading "Alley Oop" before going to school at St. Teresa. And I remember Mary Worth, the 139-year-old building superintendent of a huge apartment complex in California, when she was selling apples on Times Square, and my cousin Ted once appeared in Milt Caniff's "Steve Canyon" strip. I'm a comic strip connoisseur. But now the newspapers have crammed the strips together and made them unreadable, at least for me.

As you can plainly see, because this column is printed in 10-pt type,* I'm not very happy with Gannett's new look.

I wonder if I can renew my subscription to the *Price Hill News*?

This reprint is set in 13-pt type.

WHICH WAY TO THE HERSHEY SYRUP?

June 2000

If you are not as old as I am, and most of you aren't, you don't know what grocery stores were like back in the good old days. That's something us old curmudgeons like to say, "back in the old days." Anyway, grocery stores were a lot different than the supermarkets of today.

Your mom would give you a list, and then you would get your wagon out and pull it up to the grocery. You gave the shopping list to the store clerk and he went around and gathered your items while you stood at the counter and ate vanilla wafers out of the cookie bins. I particularly remember the pole with a handle at one end and a clamp on the other that the clerk used to get things off the higher shelves. He brought the stuff to the counter, added up the prices, bagged the groceries, threw in a couple of pieces of penny candy, and then after you paid him, he carried the bags out and put them in your wagon.

In today's modern supermarkets, you become the gatherer. You get a cart and a walk around gathering your stuff off the shelves, take it to the checkout stand, wait in line, and then pay what a computer says you owe. Some supermarkets even expect you to bag your own groceries. I draw the line at that.

I'm sure the supermarket companies consider this the best method from their point of view, and I don't argue that it isn't more efficient, but a few things bother me about these super stores.

The companies that run them obviously hire people who wander the aisles in plain clothes and watch what you buy. If you find a new item that you really like and buy it three times in a row, they make a note of this and have the store discontinue the item. If they notice that you buy a certain product all the time, they move that product around to different places in the store to make it harder to find.

I feel like a mouse in a maze looking for a hidden piece of cheese when I search the aisles for Hershey syrup. Sure, I could ask one of the employees where they put it this week, but that would be like stopping in a service station when you are lost on the highway.

Real men don't ask directions.

WHADDAYA WANTA KNOW?

July 2000

Last month we finally received a question to answer for this proposed feature. It was on the Society's voice mail, and unfortunately the caller did not identify themselves. Since this is the first and only question we have received (that we know the answer to), I decided to answer it even though it was anonymous.

The question is . . . "I heard or read somewhere that Seton High School was established around 1850. Is that possible?"

And the answer is . . .

Well, it depends on how you look at it. In 1857, the Sisters of Charity established Mt. St. Vincent Academy, after buying Judge Anderson's estate and brick mansion. The nuns erected a large new building for their school in 1858 and used the judge's mansion for their convent. They called their property Cedar Grove, which was the name of one of the nun's family home in Maryland. The school was popularly known as Cedar Grove Academy.

The nuns purchased the land and homestead of Elisha Dennison Hotchkiss in 1868 and used the house as a rectory for the school's priest. It was renamed Seton Cottage in honor of the founder of the Sisters of Charity, Elizabeth Seton. The nuns continued to purchase land around the academy, and by 1881, they owned 56 acres. In 1883, they sold most of the property around the school to developers, who began to build homes in the area. The academy became a parochial high school for girls in 1927 and is now called Seton High School.

Price Hill Day at Coney

August 2000

Price Hill Day was at Coney Island this year. It was the first time it's been there in a long, long while. I was there, and if you weren't, you missed a really lovely day. The weather wasn't so great; it was cloudy and a little cool. The crowd was a little sparse, too, but the memories were spectacular.

When we got there, we carried our baskets over to the picnic grove and reserved a table with them, just like we used to do when I was a kid. While the rest of my family went off to ride the rides, I walked over to the path that comes up from the river and passes under the stone gate with the lighthouse. This is the way we always came to Coney in the old days. I used to run up this path, through the gate and over to the pony track. My grandfather boarded the ponies in the winter, so I knew them pretty well. By the time I said hello to most of them, the rest of my family would catch up and we would continue up the path.

The Land of Oz came up next, and we always had to stop there so my little cousin could ride all the dopey rides in this area. I would ride on the Wild Mouse with him and then squirm around until somebody would give me a couple of strips of tickets and tell me to run on ahead, but to stay off the roller coasters.

I would take off, run around the Merry-Go-Round, because I knew I would have to ride that later with my cousin, and jump on the Clipper, a roller coaster later renamed the Shooting Star. Next I'd ride the Tumblebug, then cut across the mall to the Dodgems and then the Whip. From there it was a mad dash to the Wildcat, another roller coaster, maybe take two rides on it, then dash all the way back up the mall to the Sky Rockets, and from up there I could see my family coming up from the Land of Oz. When I got off the ride, I went back to them, I was almost out of tickets anyway. I knew I would have to take my cousin on the carrousel next, but only with the promise that I could go on the Clipper after that, if my uncle would go with me. After the initial burst, I would mostly stay with my family; after all, they controlled the tickets. We strolled around the park, I rode the rides as we came to them, taking my cousin on the milder ones, and taking an uncle or aunt on the ones that were thought to be too violent for me to ride alone.

At supper time, we went to the Grove and had our picnic and then returned to the Midway to play the games of chance, visit the Penny Arcade, go through the Fun House, and watch Suicide Simon blow himself up. Then it was time for the fireworks. After we watched them, we always got frozen custard, picked up our picnic baskets, and headed for the *Island Queen* to take us home.

They just don't make Price Hill Days like they used to.

Skyline Through the Years

September 2000

The other day, when I left our new building, I drove past the Skyline on Glenway Avenue. This was the original Skyline Chili Parlor.

When Nicholas Lambrinides opened in 1949, he had me paint some menu posters. This was one of the first sign paining jobs I had ever done for money. Since then I have worked off and on for Skyline and the Lambrinides for over forty years. I know, because I was in their 40th anniversary television commercial and my company had made many of the props used in the production.

Being associated with Skyline has been a lot of fun. We have collaborated on many strange projects. The Skyline Flying Club was one of my favorites. Skyline was going to buy and fly a hot air balloon. I was to manufacture specially printed kites and paper airplanes and produce a Skyline Flying Club Newsletter. We were going to sponsor kite contests and balloon rides around the tristate. We worked on this for almost a year, but it never got off the ground, so to speak. I think the insurance on the balloon was just too expensive.

I, personally, invented the "Cheese Coney." Nobody at Skyline believes me, but back in the early 1950s, I ordered some coney islands at the chili parlor on Glenway Avenue. I asked the old waiter who hardly spoke English to put some cheese on them. He vehemently refused, "No cheesea ona da coneys." I finally talked him into bringing me a side order of cheese. I put it on my sandwiches and the "Cheese Coney" was born.

In the mid-1970s, Bob Hope was having a little party in Palm Springs and wanted to serve Skyline Chili. I got together with the guys at Skyline and we shipped out a care package, actually three packages. This was before the chili company packaged their product frozen. We surrounded the chili with dry ice and packed it all in Styrofoam. I then bought a seat on a flight to Palm Springs and left the chili in the care of one of the flight attendants. I had someone in California pick it up and Mr. Hope got his Skyline without a hitch!

THE OLD MAIL BAG

October 2000

I don't really have any thing important to write about this month, so I thought I'd do what other columnists do—go to the mail bag.

We do get letters, not a lot, but at least a few. For example, many people have written to ask when we are going to print the second chapter of Obie Elberon's oral history. You remember Obie; we wrote about him in last April's issue, the April Fool issue, for those of you that didn't get that back in the spring. I'm sorry to say that Obadiah Elberon didn't really exist. His story was part of the joke.

Another writer took me to task for calling the miniature roller coaster in the Land of Oz at Coney Island the Wild Mouse. They were absolutely right, it was the Teddy Bear. I knew that, really I did; I just slipped up.

My favorite letter came from "Old-Fashioned, E-Business Girl," a member who lives in Texas. She claims to be young enough to be my daughter, but she still shops for groceries the way I did when I was a kid. She simply goes to the corner Internet store and gives them her shopping list. In a few hours a delivery boy brings everything she ordered, including fresh vegetables, right to her kitchen. She says it is very convenient and the boy would not even accept a tip. Maybe I ought to try shopping that way; they sure couldn't hide the Hershey's syrup if I could do a global search for it right from my keyboard.

Most of the letters I get are as silly as my columns, but I do enjoy reading them. If you would like to write, just send snail mail to The Old Curmudgeon, Price Hill Historical Society, P.O. Box 7020, Cincinnati, Ohio 45205-7020.

Keep those cards and letters coming, we can use them from time to time when I don't have anything to grouse about!

Editor's Note: No, we didn't skip a column. The December 2000 column follows directly after this October 2000 **Old Curmudgeon's Corner** *because for some reason we can't recall, there was no* **Old Curmudgeon** *column in the November 2000 newsletter.*

LIVE OR DIE BY THE YARD SIGNS

December 2000

By the time you read this, the elections will be over. Or will they? I'm writing this on the day after the election, and the Presidential race is still undecided. I think this is probably the most exciting thing that could have happened to two rather dull candidates.

I watched the first Presidential debate and thought it was an embarrassment. The other two were a little better, but still under-whelming. I, personally, thought both candidates were lightweights. But one of these lightweights will be running our country for the next four years, if they can straighten Florida out, that is.

The local elections are what bothered me the most this year. The television commercials run by some of our local candidates were, again in my opinion, atrocious. From dancing marionettes to Barbie dolls, from acrimonious Web sites to suggestions of astronomical bribery and so on, they were amateurish, deceiving, and in bad taste. I'd like to see all political television commercials eliminated. Let 'em live or die by their yards signs.

One way or another, it's all over. At least it's all over except the counting. And counting. And counting. But soon we can all go back to watching Wonder Woman sell eyeglasses and football players push faster access to the Internet.

PITHY MOT

Have you ever wondered why, if you send a package in a truck over the road—
      It is called a shipment.
But if you send the same package on a boat over the water—
      It is called cargo.

A New Year, Century, Millennium

January 2001

The Holiday Season has come and gone. I hope yours was a happy one. We now begin a new year . . . a new century. I remember as a boy, reading the adventures of

in the comics. Those adventures seemed rather far-fetched back then, but now, at only the beginning of the 21st century, most of his futuristic gadgets appear not to be too unrealistic, and we're still four hundred years before his time.

In my lifetime I have seen the flight of an airplane overhead go from a very unusual, exciting event to a nuisance. On television I have seen Howdy Doody sitting on Buffalo Bob's lap go to Neil Armstrong walking on the moon. I remember the game "Candy Land." Now kids play virtual reality games and massacre hundreds of aliens every day. I've seen our personal lives go from rather private affairs to open books for anyone with a computer.

I remember the nuns telling me that God knew when even the smallest sparrow fell. With all the satellites up there, now the government knows, too.

Few of us will live to see beyond this century; I personally am glad to leave it to Captain Buck.

SLIDERS AT WARP SPEED NO MORE

February 2001

I love White Castles . . . those little, square culinary delights. The perfect combination of meat, vegetables, and grain. I can remember when they cost only a nickel. Hey, it wasn't that long ago. They used to put coupons in the newspapers, you could get 24 for a dollar. You had to go to Camp Washington, because there weren't any "Castles" around Price Hill. So, I would drive down (yes, we did have automobiles back in those days) armed with one of the coupons and a buck and order a couple of dozen of the little beauties.

The thing that was so amazing about their operation was their efficiency. You could walk in and place your order, and before you could get your money out they were handing you your burgers. One night some years ago, there were a bunch of teenaged kids sitting around our kitchen. They decided that they needed some White Castles. I volunteered to go down and get them. They weren't a nickel anymore, but they were still pretty cheap. I placed my order and the cashier called out, "A hundred White Castles, three no onion." I paid the lady and moved over to a stool to wait. But I had no more than sat down when one of the waitresses plunked a cardboard box in front of me. A couple of the other girls started putting bags of burgers in the box.

"This bag has the three no onions in it," said the girl with the last bag. "Sorry for the wait." That place was the epitome of fast food.

My wife and my doctor have both told me that the "little sliders" are bad for me, so I don't eat them very often. But last week I happened to be in Cheviot around lunch time so I stopped at the White Castle out there. I noticed that White Castles now cost about ten times the original nickel, but everything has gone up, so I decided to order some. While trying to place my order, I was interrupted by a previous customer who had received the wrong order. Finally, after talking to two different ladies, I got my order in. While I waited for my order, two more customers complained about mistakes in their orders and one person got the wrong change.

I checked my order when it arrived, 13 minutes and 24 seconds after placing it, everything was right and the burgers were delicious.

What happened to the fabled efficiency? Was it only that the old White Castle in Camp Washington was so good, or is it that nobody gives a darn anymore?

BURGLARY IS NO JOKE

March 2001

Have you ever been burglarized?

It happened to me last month, and it's not a great experience.

My wife was out of town and I wasn't at home all morning. When I got home that afternoon, I found my back door smashed in and the window on the porch was broken. With only the average intelligence God gave me, I knew immediately that something was wrong.

I cautiously went into the house. It was a mess, but there was nobody lurking around. I called 9-1-1 and a policeman arrived a little while later. He went through the house with me, taking notes. Then he called headquarters to have an investigation team sent out.

They arrived and checked things very thoroughly. They were here for about three hours and returned the next morning. I was very impressed with the work of the police of District 3 and every one of them seemed genuinely concerned with my problems.

For two days, I was very busy, talking to the police and the insurance company, cleaning up, boarding up the door, and getting the window fixed. By the third day I had things in some sort of order and that's when I got depressed.

Most of what was taken was jewelry. Many of the items were keepsakes and heirlooms. They can never be replaced.

In spite of some of the things I have written in past columns, I have always believed in the basic honesty of humanity. I wouldn't dream of taking someone else's property, and I am sure most people wouldn't either. But the person or persons that broke down my back door have, sadly, changed my outlook. They have made me suspicious of the world.

I will lock my car doors whenever I'm not in it. The windows and new, steel doors in my house will also always be locked. If you should happen to have car problems in my neighborhood, don't ask to use my phone. I'm even going to lock the lower door when I'm upstairs at the Society.

Do you think I'm becoming paranoid? You're right. Not only that, I'm probably going to become a real curmudgeon.

That's sad.

A FEW EARLY APRIL UPDATES

April 2001

Last year, if you remember, we did an April Fool's issue of our PHHS newsletter. It was great fun and I think everyone enjoyed it, but it did cause some confusion. This April we decided to play it straight and not pull on your respective legs too hard. But I do have a few updates on last year's issue that I would like to pass on to you.

- The Cincinnati Recreation Department reneged on their promise to build a lighted croquet court at Carson-Covedale Park. They claim the neighbors on Benz Avenue were concerned about the possibility that sticky wickets could play havoc with their plumbing.

- The Northern Kentucky religious group has had second thoughts about turning Sieve Pontiac into a Creationist Museum because there is a bill pending before the State Legislature prohibiting the building of religious structures within 500 feet of a public school.

- Happily, the Reformed Druids are still hoping to create their seminary on the property at Glenway and Considine. The only obstacle is getting CG&E to remove all the overhead wires that cross Glenway so that the huge 30-meter-high stones can be dragged up the hill to the site.

- Mary Bazeley received her grant for funds to purchase 40 tons of mulch for the Covedale Conservatory. She has had the mulch delivered to the rear parking lot, but once again, the city has dropped the ball. The Covedale Theater is still showing movies and there are no tropical plants in evidence. (Don't say anything about the smell to those lovely folks who work at the library. They are a little touchy about it and trying to ignore it.)

- Finally, a note about Obadiah Elberon. Obadiah would have been 103 on January 3, 2001. He got up bright and early on New Year's Day. He went down to breakfast, had a bowl of oatmeal, and was heard to say, "I been eating that pap for a century. This is a new millennium, and dammed if I'll ever eat it again."

He went back to his room and died peacefully. May he rest in peace.

Learning to Play the Game

May 2001

I watch my children racing around taking their children to various sports practices and games. Soccer practice at 6:00, and the other one has a game at 6:30; it's in Sayler Park. You take the one, I'll take the other and we can meet at Sam's for supper. It's something like that every night of the week, except on weekends, and then it's even worse.

Kids today are strictly taught all the rules and strategies of various games. They start baseball at around five or six years old. They join a team that is part of a league. The league could win its division, the city, and state championships, and then wind up in some place like Paraguay playing for the world championship.

A team has several coaches plus at least one parent per child, each of whom is willing to offer advice at the drop of a hat, even if they have to drop their own hat . . .

Football and basketball are pretty much the same, but soccer is a world of its own. Apparently they practice or play every day. They play indoors and out and it seems to go on all year long. Not only does every school, church, suburb, and block have its own team, each of which has a league of its own and world champion, there are semi-professional, indoor teams, and leagues. They actually recruit 8- and 9-year-olds. I'm not finding fault with this system of learning the games, if the parents can put up with it and the kids don't burn out by 12.

But back in the "old days" . . . your first taste of sports came, much like today, when you were five or six. Your dad or an uncle or some adult brought you a ball of some kind and started throwing it at you. In self defense, you soon learned that it was better to catch the ball than to keep getting hit by it. By this time the adult got bored and left, so you called the little guy next door. He had already been pretty well bruised by his own adult so he could catch and throw the ball fairly well. The two of you tossed the ball back and forth until you could catch it almost every time.

About the time you mastered this skill, the same (or another) adult would bring you a different kind of a ball. This one was oblong and had pointy ends, and you followed the same procedures as before, so soon you and the kid next door were passing a football back and forth. The same thing happened when you got a basketball.

Soccer? Nobody ever heard of soccer. That was something you yelled when one of the little girls came into the boys' part of the playground at recess.

While you and the kid next door were going through these learning processes, the same thing was happening all over the neighborhood and soon it had to all come together. One of the slightly older kids would say, "Let's go out to Witsken's and play . . ." whichever game the season called for.

Everybody went and were divided into two teams. (How these divisions were arrived at is enough for another column.) The older kids told the younger kids where to stand and what to do and gave them their own interpretation of the rules, and then play began.

We basically learned to play baseball, basketball, and football the same way, except basketball was generally played in somebody's backyard where there was a makeshift basket nailed up on a garage roof.

We attempted to learn hockey in much the same way, but things like ice skates that fell off, the lack of proper tree limbs to use as sticks, and the fact that even in our coldest winters the ice invariably had thin spots where someone fell through, meant that it never became very popular.

By the fifth or sixth grade, our schools had regular teams with a coach and uniforms and everything. At this point we pretty much learned the real rules of the various games, and honed our skills.

Of course, at our school you had to be a server or singer to be allowed to play on the teams. My lack of ability to sing or learn a dead language prevented me from being in either of these elite groups. But as luck would have it, our coach would stop in my dad's saloon on the way to and from practice for a little pick-me-up. He was not awed by the little dictator who governed our parish, so he bent the rules and allowed me to play, not often nor too well, but enough to gain some honorable cuts and bruises, a broken collarbone, and a working knowledge of the games.

We did not get the formal training that today's youth receives. Our parents only got involved when we broke a bone or something. The professional athletes that came out of our system didn't make millions of dollars a year, except maybe Donny Zimmer—he is still in the game, you know.

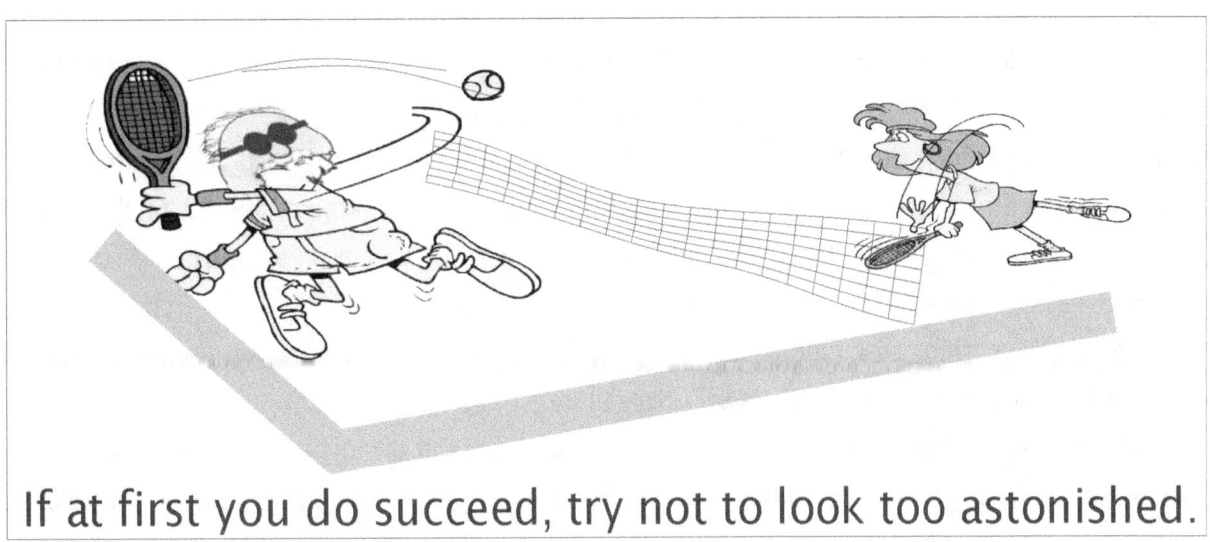

If at first you do succeed, try not to look too astonished.

THEY GOTCHA

June 2001

The high price of gasoline . . . one of today's hottest topics. It's almost two dollars per gallon. People are saying we soon won't be able to drive our cars . . . but don't you believe it. Americans will still drive everywhere they go. If the price goes up to four dollars a gallon, Americans will drive their cars.

Once years ago I left Denver, Colorado, on a little sightseeing trip. I filled my gas tank in the city with 18-cents a gallon gasoline. I ran short of gas about halfway up Pike's Peak. Luckily there was a gas station there, but gasoline was 38 cents a gallon. I was aghast, it cost more than twice as much up here on the side of a hill as it was down below. I could have turned around and coasted down to where the prices were lower. It would have been a hairy journey, but I could have made it. I didn't, though—I bought the high-priced gas.

I asked the old geezer who was pumping the gas how come he could charge so much. "'Cause I gotcha," he explained. "Folks don't realize how much gas it takes to pull this mountain, and I'm the only game in town. I get most everybody, either comin' or goin'. Damn few of you gawkers wanna navigate this long windy road on empty. I could sell my gas for a buck a gallon, but I'm a kind, considerate sort of fellow.

"Supply and demand, young fella. That's the name of the game. I got the supply and I can demand what I want for it. You want I should check the oil?"

Supply and demand, that still is the name of the game now. As long as American drivers demand the energy it takes to drive their cars, the suppliers can get what they want for it.

If you consider what we pay for other liquid items we buy, you will find that gasoline at two dollars a gallon is still one of the cheapest. I recently bought some WD40, another petroleum product. It costs $57.28 a gallon. I didn't buy a gallon, but that's what it would have cost. While sitting in the Burger King on St. Lawrence, I noticed that the orange juice I was drinking cost $1.19, or about $6.40 a gallon, and oranges grow on trees. We had dinner at a local restaurant on a Saturday evening and I noticed that they were selling martinis for the rock-bottom price of $72.00 a gallon. The jelly I had on my toast this morning cost, by the gallon, $13.76. And if you cook, I'm sure you use vanilla extract occasionally. The cheapest I found costs $57.28 a gallon.

Is there any point to this story? No, it's like comparing brussel sprouts and iron ingots, but if you start thinking about the price per gallon of things you use every day, two bucks a gallon for gasoline doesn't sound quite so bad.

Like the man on the mountain said, "I got cha." If you want it, then you'll pay for it, no matter what it costs.

MOVING DAY

July 2001

The Old Curmudgeon is moving. Moving out of Price Hill. By the time you read this, I will have already moved.

I guess this disproves the old adage that says you can't take the boy out of Price Hill.

Actually, our new place is only a mile and a tenth from the house we lived in for forty years and it's still on the same street.

I will now live in Delhi, but not for long. I have recently talked to our State Representative, Steve Driehaus, about changing the name of that little corner of Delhi to "South Price Hill." Not only will that get me back to our beloved "Hill," but I figure I will be eligible for ten thousand dollars a year in NSP funds.

Until Steve can arrange the name change, I will live just on the cusp of the "Hill," but I will still consider myself a "Price Hillian."

Sorry for the brevity of this column, but moving is time and energy consuming. I'll go longer next month, you can rest assured.

PITHY MOT

Around the Price Hill Historical Society, there are very few "spring chickens." Most of us are at least a little past prime. But did you ever wonder where the term spring chicken came from?

Way back when, farmers realized that chickens hatched in the spring were much more tender than those that had lived through the winter. Of course, when they sold the birds, they told their customers that they were all spring chickens. A customer who got an older bird, however, might complain that the bird they bought was certainly no spring chicken! Thus, the connotation "spring chicken" came to mean a person who was still in their tender years.

UTILIZING THE SUNDAY PAPER

August 2001

On a Sunday in the middle of June I woke up early, walked out, and picked up my *Enquirer*. As I returned to the house, I realized that this was the last Sunday paper I would get at this address. After forty years I was moving . . . so much for nostalgia.

I grabbed a cup of coffee and retired to the back porch to play my regular Sunday morning game of "Try to Find the Funny Papers." I always read the comics first. Mary Worth seems to have more problems than I do, so she makes my day a little brighter. I then turned to the Forum section, which always brings me back down.

On this particular Sunday I perused the rest of the paper rather quickly, so I decided to take it with me to our new house, a very fortunate decision as it turned out.

When I arrived at our new place I noticed that a very large dog had left a mess right where the move men would be walking the next day. I grabbed an ad supplement out of my paper (apologies to Michael's) and managed to clean it up.

Once inside the new place, I got out a card table, set it up, and spread the Sports section over it, then polished the silver lid of my cigar humidor.

Next I had to touch up a little area on one of the baseboards. I laid the Business section of the *Enquirer* on the kitchen counter and got out my paint and brush. I used the Tempo section as a drop cloth and did my touch up. I put my paint away and wrapped the spattered paper in the front page.

My next project was to wipe some bird droppings off the railing around the porch. I put the Metro section under the rail then scrubbed it with cleanser and the crumpled classified ads. I find the *Enquirer* more abrasive than paper towels, even more abrasive than the *Post-Times Star*.

I had been putting the pieces of the newspaper that I had used into a large plastic garbage bag. I took the remaining parts of the paper, excluding the TV schedule and the *USA Today* magazine, crumpled them up, and put them into the same bag.

This provided a nice puffy pillow. I laid down on the living room floor with the bag under my head and read the *USA Today* magazine while I waited for my wife to call with more chores for me.

This was a rare Sunday when I could find no fault with our local morning newspaper.

GOING FOR THE GOLD

September 2001

The Olympics are coming! The Olympics are coming! Everybody in town is so excited . . . at least Nick Vehr is excited, but then he gets paid to be excited.

I, personally, am dubious about our city landing the games, but if they do, how can Price Hill become involved? We could possibly be the venue for several events.

My first thought is that the pavilion at Mt. Echo would be the perfect spot to hold the Award Ceremonies. The natural beauty of the area combined with the architecture of the pavilion and the city skyline in the background would look great on international television. The lake at Rapid Run Park would be a great location for the Model Sailboat competition, and how about West Eighth Street for the Stay Behind the Traffic Lines Dash?

Mount Hope Road could host the Uphill 500 Meters. At Covedale and Rapid Run, there is a perfect spot for the Mixed Couples Freestyle Mud Wrestling event.

A ramp could be built right where the Incline used to be, for the Big Wheel Downhill. I thought we might also consider the Freehand Pistol Event, but Over-the-Rhine seems to have the edge on that one.

It was Mark Twain who said he would like to be in Cincinnati when the world ended, because the people here wouldn't know it happened until ten years after the event.

If the world ended in 2010, our city could get the games . . . by default.

PITHY MOT

Our world is full of professionals. Professional baseball, football, and soccer players. Lawyers, accountants, politicians, musicians, medicos, and on and on.

Most of us consider ourselves amateurs, but that shouldn't stop us. Just remember, it was amateurs who built the ark. Professionals built the *Titanic*.

Don't Judge People Too Quickly

October 2001

I had already written my column for this month in early September, but since the recent tragedy in New York, I didn't feel that a cute little story on the history of yo-yos was particularly appropriate. So, though I'm sure all of us have heard and read enough about this disaster, I just want to make a point about something I feel strongly about.

On December 7, 1941, the Japanese mounted a devastating sneak attack on Pearl Harbor. I was a very young boy at the time, but through the duration of World War II, I was taught to hate the Japanese as inhuman and inhumane monsters. When American citizens of Japanese descent were rounded up and locked in camps, I thought this was okay—we didn't want to let them loose to wreak more havoc on the good old U. S. of A.

I would have never guessed that less than ten years after that sneak attack, I would be a member of the Japanese Occupational Forces and living right among these supposed monsters in Tokyo. There is no doubt that there were awful people in Japan, war criminals who caused their people to hate and fight us. They taught their people that we were the monsters. But the people I met in Japan were the gentlest, most polite people I have ever known. I couldn't believe the horrific stories I had heard about them while I was growing up. I'm sure they fought hard for their Emperor, and I am sure some of them participated in some atrocious actions, as did our side, but how about all those Americans who lived in concentration camps in our country? What did they do to deserve this deprivation?

Enough war story, I'm just trying to point out that this horrible deed was done by foreign terrorists. If you see someone in the grocery or on the street wearing a turban or a veil, don't hate or revile them. They are probably good Americans, just like you, me, and those Japanese Americans who spent the Second World War behind barbed wire.

Just because they worship in a mosque and not at St. Lawrence doesn't make them bad people. God is God, whatever name you call Her. It's stupid to hate people just because they don't look like us.

In our country everyone is supposed innocent until proven guilty. Let's hope that our government can find the perpetrators of this dastardly event and take the proper actions to stamp out terrorism.

Feel anger, not hatred. Seek justice, not revenge.

Y'ALL COM BAK NOW!

November 2001

My wife and I took a late vacation this year. We went to the Outer Banks of North Carolina and had a wonderful time. Great weather, great beaches, great seafood. We were on our way home, on the last day of September, just this side of Charleston, West Virginia. We were ready to stop for the night. We had seen signs that told us the next town had at least a Holiday Inn, a Ramada, a Best Western, and a Comfort Inn. It looked like a good bet, so we pulled off I-64 at the Bourbonville exit and entered the Twilight Zone.

All the streets were one way, all the same way, and they all led to "The Mall," so that's where we went. I stopped the car in the huge mall parking lot and we looked around. There was a small Comfort Inn off to our left, but over on the other side of the expressway, we saw the Ramada and decided to go take a look at it. We drove all over the Mall's parking lot until we found a little street that appeared to go in the direction we wanted. Unfortunately it took us back on I-64, going the opposite way. I drove to the next exit and got off, planning on turning around and heading back the right way, but now I was on another limited access highway and would have to go to the next exit to turn around and then . . . the highway just ended . . . it turned into a little country road that I assumed was a detour and would get me back to somewhere.

We drove up and down hills, around curve after curve, never seeing a sign of civilization. After about twenty minutes, I saw a Sinclair gas station and grocery store. I pulled in and got out. I walked around to the grocery. There were two little boys sitting by the door. They had very white hair and little beady pink eyes. One was playing a banjo and the other a harmonica. I say playing, but actually one was just strumming up and down on the banjo and the other was just bleat, bleating into the harmonica. I spoke to them, no reply. Bleat, bleat, strum, strum. I stepped over them and went through the fly-encrusted screen door. The inside was dark. It seemed to contain nothing but cobwebs, stacks of canned Wilson's Condensed Milk, and case after case of Cleo-Cola. I walked around a corner and heard a voice coming from behind a huge stack of Tag soap. "Yer lost, ainchee?" I conceded that I was definitely lost and was trying to find I-64.

"Head on back t'away ya came, 'bout fifteen minutes, tada traffic light." Traffic light? I hadn't seen even a dead possum.

"Ittle be there. Turn left and that roadal take ya ta the Mall. Even you otta be able ta find the highway from there."

I thanked the voice, left the store (strum, strum, bleat, bleat), turned around, and started looking for the traffic light. Sure enough, about fifteen minutes later, there it was—a flashing yellow light in the

(continued on next page)

middle of nowhere. I turned left into the narrowest, darkest, twistiest road I have ever been on. Sheer drop-offs into stagnant pools on one side and sheer granite walls on the other, and one hairpin curve after another. It seemed like we drove for hours and hours and we were ready to give up, just sit there til someone found us or we starved, when I saw an old bald man on the side of the road. I stopped and told him our plight.

"Wall, iffen ya weally want to go to thet danged Mall, jes go up ta hill and turn white ever time ya gotta make a choice."

I thanked the man and drove off. My wife said, "He said turn white, well, I've been white as a sheet ever since we got on to this road." We drove on and on, always to the white, I mean right, never to the left, for another eternity. Finally we came to a crossroads where there was a red truck waiting to pull on to the road. I stopped and asked the driver if I was on the right way to "The Mall."

He allowed as how the danged place was just over the next rise, and it was. The road I was on went right into the Mall parking lot. We were saved, I thought.

We decided to just go to the Comfort Inn, we could see it from where we were. Seeing it was one thing, though, and getting to it was another. I drove across the Mall's parking lot, darted across the main one-way street into a Pier 1 Imports lot, went around through the Kohl's lot, and into a little drive that took us to the Comfort Inn.

We checked in, calmed down, changed our clothes, and decided to go to the Olive Garden for dinner. We could see the restaurant's sign from the motel parking lot. I drove through Kohl's lot around the Pier 1 and back across the street to the Mall lot. Cut across it, crossed the street again into a Goodyear tire lot, around the store through Staples lot and into the Olive Garden.

We went in, the girl at the desk told us it would be about a 15-minute wait. We decided to wait. A half hour went by, nobody left. We gave up, but as we were leaving I looked into the dining area. Nobody was moving, they were just sitting there staring at their food.

We drove through several parking lots, one of which was for a Woolworth's 10-cent store, and finally came across a roadhouse-type restaurant. We went in and were once again told that it would be about 15 minutes. After 20 minutes we left, went back to the hotel, ate some cheese and hard boiled eggs that we had in the cooler, and went to bed. The night was uneventful. We got up early and got out of there. I pulled through he parking lots, cut across the one for "The Mall," found the egress that I originally got lost on, and pulled on to I-64. While we were leaving we spotted a Holiday Inn off in the distance. The shutters were half falling off it, it had an eerie yellow glow, and there was absolutely no road leading to it.

The rest of our trip was uneventful, but when we got home and I was unloading the luggage, I noticed a message written in the dust on the back of my car.

It said, "Y'all com bak now!"

I don't think so . . .

Media's Mixed Message

December 2001

We are all probably watching more television since September 11, and I think you will agree, television is more educational than ever.

Just a couple of weeks ago, while watching *60 Minutes*, I learned where most of this country's nuclear power plants are located and the best way to destroy them.

Since then, I have learned how to smuggle weapons on to airplanes, where to buy and sell these weapons, and what airports have the poorest security systems.

I have found out how to get around the immigration laws of our country and where to get forged identification papers.

The best way to wrap and mail anthrax has been covered, and suggestions have been made that smallpox could be used for more efficient bioterrorism.

Other tidbits I have learned include the proper distance to park a truck bomb from a building for best results, how to introduce botulism into the food supply, and how to build a bomb out of everyday objects that you may have laying around.

There is more, much more, but this shows you the degree of education I have garnered from the television in the past few months.

The media has done an outstanding job of educating the public. Thank goodness the terrorists don't watch the tube.

Editor's Note: **The Old Curmudgeon's Corner** *is an opinion column, and the opinions expressed here do not necessarily reflect those of the Price Hill Historical Society or its members. For that matter, the overworked editor often does not even have the time or energy to check the facts, such as they are; she is just grateful that someone else has written it.*

THE BIRD OF TIME IS ON THE WING

January 2002

Another year has zipped by, and as I am propelled into the future at an alarmingly rapid rate, I thought I'd take a little time to reflect back on a slower era in my life, when the time between Halloween and Christmas seemed to take forever.

I think it might have been television that has warped time. Those evil rays that spew forth from all those electronic boxes shrink hours perceptively. Radio waves never did that. When I was a kid, I used to rush home, after what seemed like fourteen hours in school, and listen to the fifteen-minute radio shows that seemed like they were an hour long. Shows like "Little Orphan Annie," "Tailspin Tommy," and "Don Winslow of the Navy," along with "Tom Mix," "Dick Tracy," "Smiling Jack," "Terry and the Pirates," and "Jack Armstrong, the All-American Boy," all competed for my attention until supper time.

After supper I had to do my homework, and I always felt like that took about six hours, but after finally finishing up I would return to the radio. "Return to those thrilling days of yesteryear" and the thundering hoof beats of the great horse Silver and listen to the tales of the greatest hero of them all, The Lone Ranger and his faithful Indian companion, Tonto. After that I could have my mind clouded by The Shadow or hear the further adventures of Jack, Doc, and Reggie on "I Love a Mystery." I could listen to the stories about the Lone Ranger's nephew, The Green Hornet, and his faithful Asian companion Kato.

Somewhere in the middle of one of these programs, I would be told to go to bed. I could usually stay up through two more of those bedtime calls, but on the third one, I had to tear myself away from the radio. The grown-ups wanted to listen to "One Man's Family" or "Mr. Keen, Tracer of Lost Persons," or maybe even "Dr. IQ."

The time spent sleeping was probably normal time, sixty seconds to the minute, sixty minutes to the hour, but when the radio was on, time was elongated. During school and while doing homework, the hours seemed longer, too. Weekends were entirely different. Saturdays and Sundays apparently had only fifteen hours each. According to my calculations, during the radio era, there were 11,156 hours in a year. A normal, 24-hours a day year has 8,766 hours in it, give or take daylight savings time. The television rays squeezed that down to about 6,000 hours.

Wasn't it Einstein who said, "Time is relative"? I hope you have a *relatively* HAPPY NEW YEAR. It will be shorter than the last one.

FEBRUARY ... OUR SHORTEST MONTH

February 2002

We made it through another gala holiday season and now February, our shortest month, is upon us. For a month with the smallest number of days, February has a lot of minor holidays.

Probably by the time you read this you will have already missed Groundhog Day, the day that the little furry varmint looks for his shadow. Rumor has it that Dick Cheney also emerged from his hiding place. If he saw his shadow, we will have six more weeks of Afghanistan.

February 2 is also the Celtic feast of Imbolc (the Lactation of the Lambs) honoring the goddess Brigid (pronounced *Bree' jah*). The early Christians demoted the Celtic Brigid to sainthood, so they now call it Saint Bridget's Day. It is also known as Candlemas. Whatever it is called, it is a national holiday in Ireland.

On the twelfth of the month, we used to observe Lincoln's Birthday, and on the twenty-second, we celebrated the birth of George Washington, the father of our country. Now these have been lumped together and called Presidents' Day; it is observed somewhere between the two original holidays.

This year, Ash Wednesday falls on the thirteenth of February. This is the only day of the year that it is socially acceptable to walk around with a dirty face. Ash Wednesday is also the beginning of Lent. A time of penance for most and a time of joy for the fishing industry.

February 14 is, of course, Valentine's Day, a special day set aside to enhance the sale of greeting cards, candy, and flowers. This month you should listen for "The voice of the turtle." It should be heard in our land and then will Spring be far behind?

PITHY MOT

I am sure that you have seen an old newsreel showing Japanese kamikaze pilots boarding their airplanes prior to suicide raids on U.S. ships.

Did you ever wonder why they were wearing helmets?

Orange Barrel Attack

March 2002

Is it just me, or have you also noticed the increased number of orange barrels in Price Hill? There seem to be repair crews all over our fair suburb. That's a good thing, I guess. It proves that the city has shown some interest in our potholes, antique sewage system, tangled electric lines, and so on, but getting around can be very frustrating.

Seldom can you drive from point "A" directly to point "B" these days. You keep being stopped by those heinous orange barrels and detour signs. To get to "B," you generally have to detour over "X" to "Y" to "M," "D," and "C."

It is completely impossible for me to get to my daughter's house. She lives on a corner and both streets are almost always completely impassable. I haven't seen her in weeks. The last I heard they were living on boiled gladiola bulbs.

The situation on Cleves Pike has been peculiar, to say the least. It seems like every day they close a different section of the street. You never know where the barrels will pop up next. Thank goodness it isn't high golf season, the country club folks would be very disturbed.

As long as I'm talking about driving, I might as well bring up another annoyance. I admit I'm getting old, and as you might guess from the title of this column, a little crotchety, but have you noticed how many drivers run red lights?

Today's drivers seem to treat traffic lights just like they do stop signs—they ignore them. Just try to get across the street where Ferguson meets Glenway.

There are an awful lot of cars on the road today and everyone seems to be in a terrible hurry. Can you imagine if Witsken's dairy still used horse-drawn wagons for their deliveries? Modern drivers would just run over them.

Well, as they say, "No use crying over spilt milk."

ASK YOUR DOCTOR ABOUT TV ADS

April 2002

If you watch any television at all, you have surely noticed the plethora of prescription drug ads. The drug industry spent almost $2.5 billion on mass media advertising in 2000, three times as much as it spent in 1996. Why this big jump? In 1997, the Food and Drug Administration relaxed its rules on television advertising. I don't have any figures on what they are spending this year, but if the upward trend continues, it could easily be $5 billion. Merck Pharmaceutical actually spent more, advertising Vioxx, than Budweiser spent on beer ads. It doesn't take an Enron executive to figure out that these expenditures inflate the cost of prescription drugs.

These ads, which are extremely well produced and appealing, are basically directed at consumers, not the medical profession. They are primarily aimed at you, to suggest that you talk to your physician about replacing some drug you are already being prescribed with a more expensive, newer, not necessarily better, drug.

I wondered about how effective this strategy was, so I asked my doctor if many of his patients requested these highly advertised drugs. He told me that he did not have a lot of patients who did this, and that when they did, he tried to explain to them that if he felt these newer drugs were better for their ailments, he would prescribe them without being asked, but in most cases, the medications they were taking were just as good or better for their particular problem. However, reports from surveys by consumer groups and health care organizations have concluded that 30 percent of American patients talk to their doctors about specific, well-advertised drugs, and of these, 44 percent receive the new drug.

That is a pretty good percentage, so the ads are working, but are they working to our—the patients of America's—advantage? Let's look at two of these heavily advertised super drugs, Celebrex and Vioxx. The beautiful TV ads tell us that they are more effective at treating pain than (over-the-counter) ibuprofen. "That's absolutely not true for pain," says Robert Goodman, M.D., assistant professor of clinical medicine at Columbia University. "Vioxx and Celebrex have less gastrointestinal side effects, so there's some benefit for people with ulcers," to paraphrase Dr. Goodman, but as pain killers they are no more effective than Tylenol.

In addition to the phenomenal amounts of money the drug industry spends on mass media advertising, they employ about 90,000 marketing reps who woo doctors with free samples, lunches, dinners, sporting event tickets, free luxury vacations disguised as conventions, and so on. But I know

(continued on next page)

my doctor has not succumbed to these blandishments, because he vacations at the same place I do, and it is a nice place, but certainly not a luxury resort. Also if they were trying to bribe him, they would have replaced that shiny blue suit he always wears.

I truly believe that the drug companies need research to develop new drugs. This research expands new products that help us all live longer, better lives, though why they haven't found something to cure the common cold eludes me as much as it does them. I believe the drug companies have to make the medical profession aware of these new wonderful cures. But they should allow the doctors to tell us, the uninitiated patients, about these miracles.

There is really no need for them to move mountains together or teach a dog to do yoga just to show off a big purple pill that rises and sets as only the sun once did. I'm not going to rush out to my local pony keg to buy a case, or even a six-pack.

I have really rambled on, and I hope there is room for all the extra copy in this piece, but I feel strongly that prescription drugs are way overpriced, and that unnecessary advertising costs help to inflate the prices. I certainly didn't mean this column to even hint at medical advice. I don't know any more about medicine than do the Madison Avenue advertising moguls who produce the ads we are bombarded with. If you want medical advice, ask your doctor. That's what he's there for.

I would like to point out some of the side effects of these pharmaceutical ads. They can cause headaches, nausea, a pain in the neck, and a severe shortage of finances.

(On a personal note, I'd like to tell my doctor that I was only kidding about the suit.)

Editor's Note: The views expressed in this article are those of the author and do not necessarily reflect the views of the Historical Society or of the pharmaceutical companies.

Nothing to Complain About

May 2002

I have complained about the orange barrels all over the streets in Price Hill and about the terrible mess that MSD has made of Covedale Avenue. I have written bitter words about the abominable ads that run up the costs of prescriptions. I guess I have complained about a lot of things, but isn't that what curmudgeons are supposed to do?

As I sit here today, the sun is brightly shining, it's warm, summer is coming, and I feel great. I'm sure if I thought hard enough I could come up with something to gripe about, but instead I thought I would pass on some interesting little historical tidbits. We are, after all, a Historical Society.

Last month, April, had some pretty interesting things happen in the past.

- For instance, in April 1865, Abraham Lincoln was shot while attending a performance at the Ford Theater in Washington, DC. He died from his wound and Andrew Johnson became the seventeenth president of the United States.

- The unsinkable British luxury liner the *Titanic* did the unthinkable—it hit an iceberg in the North Atlantic and sank. That was in 1912.

- In 1947, Jackie Robinson became the first black major league baseball player. He was signed by the Brooklyn Dodgers and had a long and successful career.

- My favorite historical fact concerning April is how April Fool's Day came to be. Way back in 1582, Pope Gregory came up with a new calendar. He rather fancied it and decreed that it was the official calendar of the world. Well, one of the major changes was that the first day of the year was now January 1 instead of April 1, as it had been. News didn't get around quite as fast in those days, so a lot of people weren't aware of the change and on April 1, many of them were running around wearing funny hats and tooting paper horns. The knowledgeable people laughed at them and called them "April Fools" and that's how that got started.

A Dozen Years of PHHS

June 2002

Here it is, June of 2002—would you believe that it was twelve years ago that the Price Hill Historical Society got started? Back in June 1990, a few people decided that there needed to be a group to keep the history of the Hill alive. I think I was the twenty-first member of the new Historical Society when it was formed back then. Now, as of the first of May, the Price Hill Historical Society is 420 members strong, and we have members living all over the country.

Our group has had Home Tours, Antique Roadshows, lectures, and many other events. We have sponsored or cosponsored old-time baseball games, ice cream socials, horseshoe pitches, Parties in the Park, and even croquet matches.

It was our Society that got the Thanksgiving Day parade started again, and we are trying to keep Price Hill Day going, too . . . We have recently started having bus tours and they are very popular.

We put out a great newsletter every month, in spite of my column, and we have published a number of successful books. But the Society's crowning achievement in the past twelve years is the acquisition of our building on Warsaw Avenue to house our archives, headquarters, and an ever-growing museum of Price Hill's history. And best of all, it's paid for.

Telling the public, especially the children, about Price Hill's history and traditions has been an ongoing project. We have tried to accomplish this through classroom visits and field trips by students to see our permanent exhibits, and by installing interesting displays in various locations in our area and in the city.

Our volunteers are wonderful. They have hammered, and sawed, and painted, and scrubbed and done all manner of nasty jobs to fix up our building and the exhibits. They have filed, typed, licked stamps, clipped, sewed, cooked, carried, and computed. They have built and installed displays, provided picture mats and frames, done artwork and hundreds of other things.

The Price Hill Historical Society has done all this and more without losing sight of our primary goal, preserving the memories and glories of the past and keeping Price Hill the Finest Suburb in Cincinnati.

So congratulations to us and a pat on the back to the other 419 members for a job well done, but don't let it go to your head. There is more to do.

"No Taxation Without Representation!"

July 2002

That was the battle cry of the thirteen colonies in America who were forced to pay taxes to England with no representation in Parliament. On June 11, 1776, the Second Continental Congress formed a committee to draft a document that would sever their ties with Great Britain. The committee included Benjamin Franklin, John Adams, Thomas Jefferson, Roger Sherman, and Robert Livingston. Thomas Jefferson, considered the most eloquent and strongest writer, was selected to craft the document.

He presented his final draft to the Second Continental Congress, and after 86 changes were made, the Declaration of Independence was officially adopted on July 2, 1776. Then they had to get the clerk to write a nice clean copy of the document for everyone in the Congress to sign—which they did, on July 4, 1776.

Of course, England did not accept this gracefully. They fought had to maintain their rule over the colonies, but the Americans prevailed, and that's why we celebrate the Fourth of July.

I am sure that this story is not new to any of you, but did you notice that it took only 24 days to conceive, pass, and sign off on what was probably the most important decision our country has ever made? This is astonishing when you consider that our current representatives would take two years to decide to take a restroom break. And that our city council members can debate a street name change through most of their entire terms.

Were our ancestors stronger, more dedicated, smarter than those of today? More likely, the lack of any pay and perks and the need to get back to their farms and businesses made them more decisive.

It's a Scorcher out There!

August 2002

'm sitting in the shade of an umbrella at Philipps' Swimming Pool as I compose this deathless prose, and it's hot. It has been over 90° for a number of days.

That's okay with me, I like it hot. I would rather it be 90° than 30° anytime, and the end of June and the first part of July is the perfect time for hot weather.

If you don't happen to share my enthusiasm for the steamier temperatures we are now enjoying, consider this—it could be worse.

The highest temperature ever recorded in Ohio was 113° and we are only 28th on the list of high temperatures. Greenland Ranch, California, in Death Valley, recorded the highest temperature ever anywhere in the United States, 134° on July 10, 1913. The only continent ever having recorded a higher temperature is Africa. A temperature of 136° was recorded at El Azizia, Libya. So, it could be worse.

Go Away, It's "Adult Swim" Time!

Two states are tied for last place in the highest temperature department, one is Alaska, which is understandable, but the other is Hawaii, which seems a little strange. Both have record highs of only 100°.

Imagine if we lived on Venus. The mean temperature is 870°. Imagine what it would cost to run your air conditioner if you lived there.

Alaska is the top state for the lowest record temperature, having once recorded –80°, but Montana is second, with a record of –70°. If you are really looking for a place to cool off, you might try Mars, because it gets as low as –220° there.

Better just stay here, don't move too fast, and drink plenty of liquids. Every so often turn to your neighbor and say, "Ain't it a scorcher?

A New Jewel in Our Crown

September 2002

The Queen City has a new jewel in its crown, and that jewel is right here in Price Hill. The Cincinnati Young People's Theater company has renovated the old Covedale Theater on Glenway Avenue. In a remarkably short time, Tim Perrino, the group's director, and his gang have worked wonders on the old movie house. The central partition has been removed and a large stage built. New, attractive seats have been installed. They seemed a little unwieldy when we visited, but the sight lines are good. The interior and lobby decor is quite attractive. Everything about the project, including the clever new logo, is well done.

On July 25, the Young People's Theater group opened *West Side Story* as their first production in their new facility. It was an energetic, fast-paced performance. I thought the cast might have been a bit too large for the size of the stage, but that was so all the kids could be in it, and it's great to see so many young people get a chance to perform.

The sets were well done and set changes were smooth and unobtrusive. I thought the on-stage sound was a little uneven, but the placement and amplification of the orchestra were perfect.

Alison Park, who played Maria, was a stand-out because of her beautiful voice, but Rachel Holt, as Anita, was the show stopper. She might not have been quite as good a singer, but she has a perfect musical comedy personality. I hope we see a lot more of her at the new Covedale Center for the Performing Arts.

I thoroughly enjoyed the show and was really impressed by the theater. Congratulations to Tim Perrino and all who helped him and the CYPT accomplish this remarkable feat.

Footnote: I recently heard that Tim had quite a few complaints from people who tried to get tickets for the first show, only to find that all the performances were sold out. All I can say is "Way to go, CYPT" — that's what I call a good kind of complaint. I'm sure you are going to need to order your tickets early for CYPT performances so you won't be disappointed. I look forward to future productions and hope all your performances in the future generate the same complaint!

"BREAK A LEG!"

Our Local Destruction Zone

October 2002

What in the world is going on? Covedale Avenue has been a disaster area for the better part of a year. The road was almost impassable for many months, and so were several of the side streets—Heuwerth Avenue still seems to be closed completely. Rumor has it that they finally paved Covedale and Western Hills when I was out of town, but there is still a lot of work to be done to put the neighborhood back the way it was before this whole project started.

I assume that MSD is in charge of the project, but they have turned the work over to an independent contractor and apparently don't even supervise what is going on.

Over the past several months, they have managed to disrupt the neighborhood's gas service several times and have cut into water mains on at least three occasions. They have poured concrete in many places, only to tear it out almost before it dries. They have dug ditches in the middle of the street without notifying the home owners and without putting barricades or even traffic cones around them. I know of at least four cars that have backed into these unmarked ditches and needed to be towed out. It's a wonder that anyone who lives around Covedale still has a drivable automobile.

The people doing the construction project seem to work on some part of it for a while and then get bored and move on to something else without ever finishing anything.

They did finish tearing down the buildings near Ralph Avenue and they did manage to put in the retention basin or whatever it is. They sodded, seeded, and landscaped the area. Now I notice that they have run over the bushes, cut down the trees, and dumped gravel, fill dirt, pipes, equipment, and construction debris all over the area. The trees and bushes that are left are all dead, not to mention the grass (what is left of it). The only plants that seem to be growing well are weeds—some of them are taller than small children now.

I think I saw a movie about a situation just like this when I was a kid. I can't remember the name of it, but it starred three popular actors of the time: Larry, Curly, and Moe.

You can bet that Observatory Road or Erie Avenue wouldn't stay torn up for this long, and they probably have living plants on city-owned property around there, too. If you are as tired of this situation as I am, call City Hall and tell them so!

GIVING FIDO A WAG

November 2002

Last month, George W. Bush came to Cincinnati and gave a speech. Our fair city pulled out all the stops. They set up 800 matching chairs in the rotunda of the Union Terminal and then filled them with 800 well-dressed invited guests.

Only about one percent of these guests were from west of Vine Street.

The invited guests obviously practiced the standing ovations and were cued when to perform (almost as if the nun with the clicker was there at the back of the aisle; their timing was flawless).

Not only were the inside guests beautifully arrayed and attentive, the protesters outside were equally photogenic. It looked to me like the protestors had been hand-picked, too. They were more casually attired but seemed to be as well rehearsed. They dutifully stayed on the sidewalk and carried nicely printed signs with politically correct slogans, while quietly chanting nonsense rhymes. The whole performance was very sanitary and well produced.

We, the taxpayers, spent a great deal of money bringing the President and his entourage here so the city could showcase itself and enhance its national image. Unfortunately, the proceedings came across stiff and overproduced. President Bush didn't add much with his reiteration of everything he has been saying for the past couple of weeks. Apparently it didn't impress the national TV networks either. None of them bothered to cover it.

I don't mean this article to be political. I personally think Mr. Bush is doing the best he can, probably better than his opponent could have done. He is certainly a more moral man than his predecessor (faint praise). I just thought the whole thing was a poor idea which was poorly done. I agree with President Bush that Saddam Hussein is a threat to the world. I think President Bush Sr. missed the boat in not eliminating him when he had the chance.

But all this war talk now, seems like wagging the dog. I think George W. is trying to take our minds off the economy.

Oh, did I mention that only about one percent of the invited guests were from west of Vine Street?

Editor's Note: The **Old Curmudgeon's Corner** *is an editorial column and does not necessarily reflect the opinions of the Price Hill Historical Society, its members, or even the editor of this newsletter. We welcome submissions from all our members.*

Beware: Gas Stations Can Be Detrimental to Your Health as Well as Your Pocketbook!

December 2002

The fluctuating price of gasoline is enough to make a grown man cry.

I used to buy my gasoline in the middle of the week when the prices were lower. Lately, the gas prices still seem to bounce around, but now they may go down, if they go down at all, on the weekends. You have to watch 'em like a hawk. Whenever I see that the price of gas is under $1.36, I fill up my tank.

I think one of the reasons that the price of gasoline is so high is because the service stations have to hire an extra person just to change the price signs.

The price of gasoline is bad enough, but now we are being warned that we could blow ourselves up if we're not careful when filling our tanks.

It seems that our bodies are full of static electricity and it is always possible that a spark could be created when we touch the pump nozzle to the gas tank filler. Then, that spark could cause the gasoline to explode, and if you are the one standing there sparking you could be in big trouble.

To avoid blowing yourself up every time you top off your tank, just touch the metal of your car after getting out and before taking hold of the pump nozzle. This will discharge any static electricity.

If you get back in the car while the gas is pumping, be sure to touch metal again before you remove the nozzle.

You don't want to earn the nickname "Sparky."

"I Was in My Workshop and I Got an Idea"

January 2003

I was watching a movie on the telly the other night and happened to see a really terrible commercial. It was very faded and poorly done and advertised an invention service. While I finished watching the movie, that commercial must have been repeated at least half a dozen times. It was so bad it made me wonder just how many terrible commercials we are exposed to. I guess you could say that they are all bad, but they do pay for all the programs we watch. But if you are like me, you probably just don't pay much attention to them.

Well, I decided to pay close attention for awhile and look for those ads that really annoy me. I started my research and began writing my column. Before I knew it I had written enough to fill three pages of the newsletter, and that would never do. I wrote scathing reports on big birds looking for shell-shaped islands, and of course on all the "pill" ads. You know how I hate them.

I took the sleazy guy who lies about the price of his prescription glasses to task, as well as the insurance-selling duck. Wrote about the girl with St. Vitus's Dance sitting in the car, the make of which I have never discovered, and the little kid who stands in the middle of traffic and says "Zoom, zoom."

Then there is the fellow who is deeply in debt, makes one phone call, then drives off for a picnic in a $40,000 SUV.

I went on and on about business owners who do their own commercials. Lee Iacocca and Dave Thomas were great, but the rest of them need a lot of help. The most annoying thing about commercials is the number of times they repeat them in the same program. At any rate, I decided that I had gotten carried away. I decided to scrap it all and wish everyone a Happy New Year instead.

We had a good year here at the Society. I hope that 2002 has been good for all of you and that the New Year will bring all of you contentment and prosperity. Happy New Year!

THROW YOUR MONEY IN A HOLE

February 2003

Recently everyone was excited about a lottery prize of 315 million dollars, which was won by a seemingly nice man who gave a lot of his winnings to various charities. He spread some of it around his family and put some of his laid-off employees back to work. I think that's great, the only thing that bothers me is where did that 315 million dollars come from?

Obviously, it came from the sale of lottery numbers. In order for the lottery to make a profit, and all gambling makes a profit for someone, they have to take in more than they pay out. A lot of people plunked down a lot of money with very little chance of winning.

I hear people talking about going to the gambling boats, and occasionally I hear about how they won money, but only occasionally. The boats always make a profit, so most of the boaters lose.

A lady once told me a story about taking a bus to Cherokee, North Carolina, to play Bingo. Unfortunately, she spent $300 on some kind of gambling "pull aparts" on the bus and didn't have enough money left to buy bingo cards.

When I was a boy, I think the primary occupation in Price Hill and Cheviot was bookmaking. Bookmakers did not print manuscripts and bind them. They took bets on horse races. My dad owned a saloon, and most of his friends made book. They were colorful characters and had nicknames straight out of a Damon Runyon story. There was Doughboy, Walking Man, High Pockets, and his brother Low Pockets. There was a Tiny, who weighed about 350 pounds, Sunshine, Glenmore Charlie, and others. They all made a profit.

The customers in the saloon were the bettors, but they were not the only ones. The green grocer around the corner didn't drink, but he stopped in every morning to place his bets. As did the haberdasher, the butcher next door, and the barber. I don't think we had a candle maker, but if we did, I'm sure he stopped in from time to time. These people seldom made a profit.

I was tending bar one Saturday morning and two regular customers, Pat and Mike, came in for a beer. They were headed to the "Ranch," a bookmaking establishment out on Crookshank. Pat said to Mike, "I hope I break even today, I can't afford to lose anything." I asked him why he didn't just not bet. He looked at me like I was feeble-minded.

My dad dealt with those people day in and day out. He could certainly see who was making the profit, but he bet the horses, too. He usually bet "sure things" and "hot tips," which occasionally won. So his profit margin never got to far into the red, but it was seldom in the black.

He gave me some good advice. He told me to dig a hole in the backyard, and every time I got the urge to make a bet, to throw the money into the hole. Do this for fifty years. The money in the hole could blow away or deteriorate or be eaten by squirrels, but if there is anything left at all, you will be ahead.

Remember: February 16 is "Do a Favor for a Grouch Day."

CHERRY BLOSSOMS AND KARAOKE

March 2003

Japan, that wonderful country that brought us cherry trees, sushi, Godzilla, the Iron Chef, karaoke, and, of course, World War II, is in serious trouble.

We here in the United States worry about George W's need to get Saddam Hussein, because his daddy missed him, and are concerned over the shortage of duct tape . . . people are taping shut their windows to protect them from Arab gas and bugs.

I'm not making light of the threat of terrorists, I just think that some of the bizarre preparations people are making are pretty silly.

Remember when we were drilled to get under a table or a desk if we thought there was going to be an atomic attack? A fat lot of good that would have done, just like the duct-taped windows.

We are also a little concerned about North Korea and their nuclear bombs, but we still have some tables and desks to crouch under.

But back to Japan . . . It seems like the karaoke fad is fading. Karaoke blossomed into a global, multi-billion-dollar business after its 1971 inception in Japan.

Karaoke, for the ignorant, unsophisticated oafs who don't hang out in bars and lounges, is a machine that plays music and allows usually slightly piflicated customers to sing along with it. It's not a pretty thing, but it has been quite popular.

However, in the past five years, there has been a worldwide slump in both the number of karaoke bars and singers.

The industry is devastated. They are currently trying to adapt karaoke to cell phones and automobile radios.

I think if they tried to put it in shower heads, they might have a winner.

A GOOD SONG'S MEASURE

April 2003

As I sit here writing this, our country is on the brink of war. By the time you read this column, our service men and women could be embroiled in deadly combat.

Many people in this country are opposed to the war. Others think that it is necessary. President Bush is among those in the latter group. So we are probably in the middle of a conflict.

In the last half of the twentieth century, our country has been involved in several other unpopular wars. Many protested the Korean Conflict and every confrontation since.

There is nothing funny about war. Yet this column is supposed to be humorous. To find anything amusing, I have to go all the way back to World War II. It was not an amusing time to be sure, but I remember two things that seemed funny to me.

Do you remember that "Lucky Strike Green Has Gone to War"? I could just picture some big tub of water where they soaked the green out of the cigarette packs and then threw uniforms in to be dyed.

How about Mock Apple Pie? There was a recipe for an apple pie that substituted crackers for apple slices. I always wondered what they did with the apples to help the war effort.

I have often said that the only reason the Second World War was more popular than any since, was because of the songs.

"Praise the Lord and Pass the Ammunition," "In Der Fuehrer's Face," and "Johnny Got a Zero." Now those were some great songs. And who could forget "Remember Pearl Harbor"? They don't write them like that any more.

The only song I remember from the Korean Conflict (my war) was "China Night." The lyrics started out, "She Ain't Got No Yoyo." Hardly inspiring.

Nothing memorable came out of our other disputes either. "Vietnama-Mama," "My Gypsy Qatar," and "Grenada On My Mind" never stirred the fires of patriotism.

Mr. Bush, what you need is not France's approval, nor blessings from the U.N.

Find another Irving Berlin or Johnny Mercer.

WAR AND PEACE AND A HOME TOUR

May 2003

The war in Iraq is still raging as I write this. Apparently, things are going well, if any part of a war could be considered going well.

The media coverage has been overwhelming. I only watch the war news from 7:45 to 8:00 every morning. I find that I hear anything that is new in those fifteen minutes. The news for the rest of the day consists of "Talking Heads" repeating what I heard in the morning.

I am patriotic enough to be pleased that we are winning, but I still question Mr. Bush's intent.

Peace, ah, there we have another quandary. When we win this war, and we will win it, will there be peace? I rather doubt it.

There will be a new government in power in Iraq. It will, surely, not be as inhumane as Saddam's rule. I worry that the new ruling party will at least be inept, if not corrupt, no matter who sets it up.

Will there then be peace? What about Syria, is that our next objective?

I don't pretend to understand President Bush's motives. I served proudly in the Armed Forces, but I am not comfortable with our country being the aggressor.

On a brighter note, our last Home Tour was a great event. The weather was a little chilly, but I had a great time. Early in the day I walked around taking pictures. Occasionally, I rode on the trolley and talked to our guests. Everyone I talked to said they were having a wonderful time and all the houses were beautiful.

I managed to talk to several of the people who were sponsors of the event. They told me that we had certainly done a nice job and how cooperative the home owners had been.

Later in the day I helped out at Bud Callaway's house. If you missed this one you probably missed the highlight of the tour. Bud and his family collect antiques, and I have never before seen such a collection. It would take a week to see everything in the house.

About four o'clock, my leg started bothering me, so I went back to Elder. While I was there, I was surprised at the number of people who stopped in to tell us how wonderful the tour was.

Our event was a great success, and I hope it took people's minds off the current strife our country is involved in, at least for a little while.

Many of the people I talked to asked me to express their thanks to the folks who worked so hard to make the Spring Home Tour such a success.

To that I would like to add my own thanks and, I am sure, the thanks of everyone in the Society, to all our volunteers, sponsors, and home owners who helped to make the Cedar Grove Home Tour such a great success.

A Classic Ohio Antique

June 2003

At the tail end of last month, May 29, to be precise, Bob Hope was 100 years old. I think that qualifies him for antique status. His wife Delores was 93 on May 27, so she can probably be considered an antique, too.

Bob Hope was born in Eltham, England, in 1903. He and his parents came to the United States in 1907, and he grew up in Cleveland, Ohio, so it seems fair for Ohio to claim him as its favorite son.

I certainly don't have to write about his world-renowned accomplishments; everyone has heard about them. He has won so many awards, accomplished success in every field of entertainment, and helped such numerous charitable organizations, that it is hard to believe one man could do so much in the short span of 100 years. On top of all that, he has entertained our service men in every war from World War II through Desert Storm.

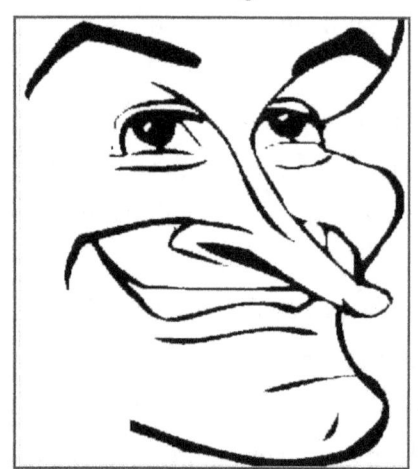

As I said, you know all about that stuff. I would like to tell you about his association with Cincinnati. There is a boys' home here in Cincinnati called The Bob Hope House on Miles Road, and it has been one of Hope's favorite charities for a long time.

In the early 1970s, Bob put on an annual variety show here in Cincinnati. He would arrange for numerous celebrities to perform gratis in the show and the proceeds went to the Hope House. I got involved in helping to produce the shows in a roundabout way, and that's how I met Bob Hope.

Such stars as Mark Hamill, Loretta Lynn, Jane Russell, Marilyn Maxwell, Charo, Glen Campbell, and many others appeared in one or more of the shows. Perry Como and Minnie Pearl were also regulars and two of the nicest people in the world. Delores Hope always sang a couple of songs in the show, another really nice lady. The shows were very entertaining, and there were always good crowds down at what was then called the Coliseum.

Bob would come to town a few days before the show. He would always visit the Hope House and then look for some place to play golf. He also liked to walk around town early in the morning, usually around 2:00 am. One night he came upon a vagrant sleeping in an alley and started to tell him jokes.

I remember that whenever Hope wasn't talking, he was humming. He hummed incessantly.

Before one of the shows, my daughter was called on to prepare Mr. Hope's script. She went to the Hopes' suite at the Netherland Plaza (they always had the "President's Suite" there), and he answered the door in his pajamas, even though it was middle of the afternoon. He gave her a long typewritten list of jokes and each one was numbered. Then he gave her a list of numbers and told her that those were the jokes he wanted to use and that she should type them up and arrange them in proper order. She told me that she made a few changes to the jokes and that he didn't notice. Her first editing gig, and she's still doing it today.

Since we all pitched in to do whatever needed to be done to put on these shows, my daughter also tended bar at the hospitality suite at the hotel, which was set up for the entertainers. Charo drank a lot of orange juice, and I don't think we'd better go into what other people drank, or how much.

My youngest daughter still remembers meeting Luke Skywalker (Hamill), and when she met him again years later, when she was working at Disney World, he remembered the Hope Supershow in Cincinnati. It was that kind of event, and Bob Hope didn't just call in favors from entertainers to perform. They seemed to genuinely enjoy doing the favor for him.

During the shows, Bob would stand off in a corner by himself, humming. You would almost think he was nervous. How could anyone who had performed in front of kings, queens, eleven presidents, millions of service men and women, and other countless millions of people, be nervous performing in front of only fifteen thousand people in Cincinnati, Ohio?

There were two other things that Bob Hope loved about Cincinnati, Montgomery Inn ribs and Skyline Chili. He probably still has shipments of these two items regularly sent to him out in Palm Springs. Maybe it was that good food that has kept him going to reach his centennial.

Bob Hope, antique or not, is truly one of this country's and Ohio's real treasures.

Happy Birthday, Bob!

It's Not Easy Being a Curmudgeon

July 2003

Being a curmudgeon carries a lot of responsibility. One is expected to be a grouch and a complainer. I do my best, but it seems like an unending job.

Restaurants are a perfect example. A curmudgeon is obligated to complain if the service is poor or if the food is not prepared properly. Actually, everyone should complain about bad service or food.

I have done work for most of the restaurants in town and I know that the management appreciates your comments, so they can improve things.

I once considered writing a book, "Tips for Waitresses." It would have pointed out things a good server should know. One of my pet peeves is when waitresses or waiters stand around gossiping. Another is when they bring your change in large bills so you can't work out a proper tip.

Last month, on our way home from vacation, we ate in a very nice restaurant. Unfortunately, our waitress was serving too many tables and as a result, the service was poor. I didn't say anything to the waitress, but I did tell the hostess that she was way too busy and as a result our service was poor.

In the same restaurant I noticed that there was only one busboy covering the whole place. As we were leaving I gave the boy a two-dollar tip and told him that I thought he was overworked. I made sure that the hostess saw me and heard me.

When you spend your money in a restaurant, you should expect good service and properly prepared food. You shouldn't have to ask to have your coffee refilled, and your food should be served hot and look appetizing.

By the same token, good service and especially tasty dishes should be complimented. Even curmudgeons do that. I always pay a compliment to the Grape Pie at Habig's, the Ribs at Circle K, and the Eggs Benedict at Dee Felice's.

Almost any decent restaurant in Lexington serves a Kentucky Hot Brown worthy of praise, and I always pay my respect to the beignets at the Café du Monde, in New Orleans, I just never wear dark clothing when I eat them.

While we're on the subject of restaurants, I should mention that it's not a good idea to recommend a restaurant to anyone. The best place you have ever eaten will invariably screw up when someone you recommended it to eats there.

Just remember, if something in a restaurant is particularly good, compliment it, but if something displeases you, complain.

We curmudgeons can't do all the work.

QUESTIONING THE CURMUDGEON

August 2003

It's July when I'm writing this, the peak of those lazy, hazy days of summer. I don't feel like thinking about something to gripe about. So, in the tradition of columnists everywhere, I am going to answer some of the letters I have received.

Someone wrote me recently about the complaining I did about television commercials. They suggested that these commercials are what pay for the programs they interrupt. Probably the writer was from "Quality Mattress" or "Furniture Fair." I know that the commercials are a necessary evil, but do they have to keep running the same ones over and over?

Another writer took me to task for what I had to say about George Bush Jr.'s visit to Cincinnati, way back in October of 2002. Claimed I said nobody from the West Side was invited to Bush's perfectly organized speech. They said that they, West Siders, were there and that they were sure that others from this side of town were probably invited. Since the PHHS is strictly a nonpolitical group, I am not going to get into that. Maybe the people from over here just had enough sense not to go.

A lady wrote me about the gambling boats. Said they were fun places to while away an afternoon and that we should have one in Cincinnati because they generated a lot of tax revenue. Okay, they generate a lot of taxes, but they also generate a lot of profits for the boats, and I don't hear about a lot of winners. If she doesn't want to travel all the way to Indiana to while away an afternoon, why doesn't she go down to the public landing and throw quarters into the river, one by one? She'll get the same results she would have gotten if she traveled all the way to Rising Sun and put them into the slot machines.

A gentleman, probably about my age, wrote me about the "bookies" of Price Hill. He fondly remembered Monty, the walking book. I remember Monty, too. He used to walk Warsaw and Glenway every day that the tracks were open. He would take bets from the people on the streets. Bets of a quarter, maybe fifty cents. If you won, you could always count on Monty to find you the next day and pay off. If you lost, which was usually the case, he would give you a smile and wish you better luck next time.

Gee, this was a pretty easy way to write a column. I can see why all the "Big Boys" do it from time to time.

A Driver's License Is a Privilege, Not a Right of Passage

September 2003

Out in Santa Monica, California, last month, an elderly man drove a Buick into a crowded outdoor market. Ten people died and another forty were injured as a result of this accident. The driver had a good driving record and was not under the influence of drugs and alcohol; he simply got confused and hit the accelerator instead of the brake.

This could have happened to anyone, but this particular driver was eighty-six years old. Older drivers occasionally get into serious driving accidents, but this sort of thing happens to younger drivers, too. Older drivers actually have much better driving records than younger drivers.

This terrible accident has prompted renewed efforts to require special driving tests for the elderly. I am an older driver so you would think that I would be opposed to this testing, but I'm not. I think it is a good idea but I would carry it a little further. I think any driver who gets a moving violation should have to take a test, as well as drivers found at fault in an accident. Anyone caught driving under the influence of drugs or alcohol should lose their license for a year and then be required to pass the test before they get their license back.

The driver's tests should be more stringent than the fairly easy tests currently being given. If you drive, you have certainly noticed the number of poor or careless drivers there are on the streets these days. Many drivers pay little or no attention to stop lights and absolutely no heed to stop signs. They drive too fast, weave in and out of traffic, and pay absolutely no attention to the yellow lines in the street.

Driving an automobile should be a privilege, not a right of passage. Perhaps if the testing was tougher, the drivers would be better. Maybe, eventually, driving conditions would improve for everyone out there in their cars, trucks, and SUVs.

The best way to have better drivers is to raise the performance of the drivers. To do this we need to raise the level of the initial testing and these initial tests should be followed by periodic testing of all drivers, young and old.

I guess this was more serious than my columns often are, but this is definitely a problem that needs to be solved, with more cars on the road every day.

Greatest Thing Since Sliced Bread

October 2003

Bread is the staff of life and has been around for a long, long time. During the Stone Age, they made solid cakes from stone-crushed wild barley and wheat. In Egypt, loaves of bread were found in ancient tombs. These loaves were baked over 5,000 years ago. They even found evidence of a bakery in the excavation of an ancient Egyptian town.

A bakers' guild was established in Rome around 168 B.C. And by the Middle Ages, bread was essential. It was practically the only thing the peasants had to eat. Even through the Renaissance, bread was a necessity. When the poor people cried out for bread, Marie Antoinette suggested they eat cake. The lack of bread was not the only reason, but a revolution started. Marie lost her ability to eat cake as well as bread.

From the Middle Ages through the demise of Miss Antoinette, bread was made from all kinds of grain. It was even made from potatoes.

These breads were coarse and tough. They had thick, hard crusts. Probably half the flavor of these breads came from the dirt picked up while the grain was being ground.

Frederick Rohwedder, in 1928, perfected a machine that would slice and wrap a loaf of bread. A baker in Battle Creek, Michigan, was the first to start using this machine.

Wonder Bread, a company that was already wrapping their bread in waxed paper, started using the machine and was soon selling their product from grocery shelves.

Other bread companies adopted the process and sliced bread became easily available to all at a reasonable price.

In 1943, the government ordered bakeries to stop slicing bread. Just like Lucky Strike Green, sliced bread had gone to war. Public outcry was so intense that the ban only lasted three months.

Fairly recently, a lot of chi-chi bread stores have been springing up. They sell breads that might have been made in the Middle Ages. They are coarse and have hard crusts. On top of that, they are very expensive.

I have no desire to return to the Middle Ages, no nostalgia for the Renaissance, and I don't want my bread tough and chewy. I *like* "Air Bread." Give me a good old loaf of Wonder, the greatest thing since, well—since sliced bread.

HOW WE GOT HERE, MORE OR LESS

November 2003

When the monkeys first came down out of the trees, the first thing they noticed was that walking around on the ground wore away their tails. This created something of a problem. Without tails, they could no longer safely climb around the trees, so they became rather easy prey for other animals. To gain a little security, and to keep the rain off, they started living in caves.

To make these caves more livable, they eventually started painting pictures on the walls. Thus Art was born. The better painters soon were receiving high praise for their work and were singled out to create more and more masterpieces and the less talented would watch in awe as these masters worked. Art became Ritual. It wasn't long before Ritual progressed to Religion, and Religion, reluctantly or possibly inadvertently, spawned Science, and Science brought forth Big Business.

Big businesses buy up smaller ones and then merge with other large businesses until they become huge conglomerates, and control vast quantities of the world's resources.

Big business will someday rule the world, if their top executives don't run off with all the assets, as has happened several times lately.

If you think that large corporations could never rule the world, think again. Our country is involved in an armed conflict that has almost completely destroyed a small country. Of course, the United States, with our tax money, will hire big businesses to rebuild the country. Do you honestly believe that the lobbyists for those same large corporations didn't push pretty hard to get the war started?

Even here in Cincinnati, Mike Brown of the Bengals demanded ransom to keep his rather deplorable football team here. Several other corporations also have made exorbitant demands of the city, just to keep their companies here. Apparently we will pay, just so there will be people still in town to eat their lunches at the downtown Wendy's, another rather large business. (You might notice that the mega-business in the fast-food industry, McDonalds, gave up on the downtown Cincinnati a few years ago. I'm not sure what that means.)

I am afraid that if the current trends continue, the few of us that survive will be back living in caves. I may be better off than most of you, because I have had experience painting pictures on walls.

Editor's Note: These views are those of the Curmudgeon, with a little nudge from author Tom Robbins, and do not necessarily represent the views of the Price Hill Historical Society or its members.

WHAT WAS UP 100 YEARS AGO

December 2003

This year, 2003, is rapidly coming to an end. Like most years, it has had some momentous events. Maybe more than some years in the past, but it is the past I want to write about—one hundred years in the past to be exact.

One hundred years ago this month, the airplane was invented. That was truly a momentous event. Today airplanes fly at incredible heights, travel unbelievable distances, and carry huge cargoes. These marvels of flight now exist because two brothers from Dayton, Ohio, put together some sticks and canvas and made the resulting contraption fly through the air.

A lot of things have changed since that day the two bicycle repairmen flew through the air with the greatest of ease:

- In 1903, only 14 out of 100 homes had bathtubs. Think about that tomorrow when you are taking your nice warm shower.
- Most women only washed their hair once a month and used borax or egg yolks for shampoo.
- There were only 8,000 automobiles in the entire United States. Sometime when you are stuck at the traffic light at Prout's Corner, you can probably count that many cars in front of you.
- Sugar only cost four cents a pound. Eggs were fourteen cents a dozen and coffee was fifteen cents a pound, but you couldn't buy sliced bread . . . sliced bread, like crossword puzzles, canned beer, and iced tea, hadn't been invented yet.
- Coca Cola had been invented and in 1903, it actually contained cocaine. Marijuana, heroin, and morphine were available over the counter at the corner drugstore. They were considered guardians of mental and physical health.
- The average life expectancy in the United States was only 47. (Thank goodness we have improved on that. Just imagine how that would cut into the membership of the Price Hill Historical Society.)

So much for 1903 . . . I wish all of you a happy and prosperous 2004.

"Hot Dog!"

January 2004

The holidays are over, so I am in a rather placid state of mind. Instead of complaining this month I'm going to tell you about something I really like . . . HOT DOGS!

July is National Hot Dog Month, so this is not exactly a timely article, but just the thought of hot dogs warms my heart. What better time to write about them than during the chilly part of the year.

The hot dog is a sausage. Sausages have been around at least since the ancient Greeks. During the Middle Ages, Johann Georgehehner, in Frankfurt-am-Main, developed a sausage called a frankfurter. About the same time in Vienna, called Wien in German, a similar sausage originated. This sausage was called a wiener. People thought the sausage looked like the little German breed of dog used for hunting badgers, so they started calling the sausages "dachshunds."

In 1871, a German immigrant named Charles Feltman began selling the sausages on milk buns with sauerkraut and mustard on them at Coney Island in New York City.

That is what probably gave Nick Lambrinides the idea of topping a wiener with chili and onions, back in 1942, and why he called this Skyline delicacy a "coney island."

In 1893, at the Columbian Exposition in Chicago, the sausages were sold, without a bun, and were a big hit. At the St. Louis World's Fair in 1904, Arnold Feuchwanger sold wiener sausages and provided white gloves to his customers so they wouldn't have messy hands. People began taking the gloves home with them. Feuchwanger prevailed upon his brother-in-law, a baker, to make a sausage-shaped bun. Soon people all over the country were eating wiener sausages on long soft rolls.

How, you ask, did these tasty little sausages become known as "hot dogs"? Credit for the name goes to Thomas "Tad" Dorgan, a sports cartoonist for the *New York Journal*. He was in the press box at the New York Polo Grounds on a particularly chilly day in April of 1901. During the baseball game no one was buying ice cream, so an enterprising concessionaire started selling sausages on rolls, calling out "Red hot dachshund sausages!" They were a big hit. Tad Dorgan drew a cartoon of a barking sausage steaming in its roll, but he didn't know how to spell "dachshund," so he titled the cartoon "Hot Dog!" and the name, obviously, caught on.

WHATEVER HAPPENED TO LITTLE ORPHAN ANNIE?

February 2004

A new publisher took over the *Cincinnati Enquirer*, our morning paper, about six months ago. Since then the paper has changed considerably. The front page and national news have been trivialized. The local and sports pages have been sanitized. Recently the paper dared to change the comics. They have taken out the ones I read and replaced them with poorly drawn, inane, and less than funny comics.

They even got rid of "Mary Worth." Do you realize that strip started in 1934, as "Apple Mary"? It was one of the first strips created by a woman, Martha Orr. The strip was a view of the effects of the Depression. Mary Worth, aka Apple Mary, sold apples out of a pushcart in New York City. She was an old woman even then and that was seventy years ago. Maybe it was time for her to retire.

There were other great old comics that we never see any more. The first comic strip, "Hogan's Alley," appeared in the *New York Morning Journal* in 1892. It was created by Richard Felton Outcault. The first comic strip I remember was "Alley Oop," by V.T. Hamlin. It started in 1933. Does anyone remember "Nancy"? That strip was drawn by Ernie Bushmiller. Nancy was sort of a Cathy as a child.

The great adventure strips "Kerry Drake," "Rex Morgan," "Brenda Starr," "Mandrake," "The Phantom," and my favorite, "Terry and the Pirates" by Milt Caniff, are all gone now. "Prince Valiant," the most exquisitely drawn comic by Hal Folter, also seems to have disappeared.

There were some great funny strips, too. "The Katzenjammer Kids," "Bringing Up Father (Jiggs and Maggie)," "The Little King," "Betty Boop," "Peanuts," "Pogo," and "Popeye" have all gone away.

"Blondie," started in 1931 by Chic Young, is still around, but whatever happened to "Little Orphan Annie"? Talk about a famous comic strip, not only were Annie and Sandy, and Daddy Warbucks, Punjab, and the Asp famous in their own comic strip, they were also on the radio, in movies, and even in a Broadway musical. "Little Orphan Annie" was created by Harold Gray in 1924.

There have been a lot of great comic strips that I have enjoyed over the years, but the newest crop in the *Enquirer* are not to my liking

At least they could bring "Mary Worth" out of retirement. I think the old girl has a few good years left in her.

"SPYING" AT THE MOVIES

March 2004

I'm a spy! Most of you probably didn't know that, but I *am* a spy.

I spy for the movies. Oh, I don't have anything to do with what actually appears on the screen. I check out the theaters. I make sure that everyone who works there is doing what they are supposed to be doing and doing it correctly. Usually, I pass out a few cash awards to those that are doing a particularly good job. It's a nasty job, but someone has to do it.

I go to the movies pretty often and I am reimbursed for everything I spend. That includes popcorn, soft drinks, and candy. Unfortunately, I don't really like popcorn and I have a childhood phobia against carrying a soft drink into a theater, thanks to Mr. Penn at the Overlook Theater. I usually buy a couple of bags of overpriced candy and stick them in my pocket only to find them all melted when I get home. As I said, I get paid back all of what I spend. I guess this sounds like a pretty nice job, free movies and all, but there are some drawbacks.

When you don't have to pay for something, it can lose its value. I have found myself walking out of movies before they are half over. In the past year I gave up on "Harry Potter," "The Lord of the Rings," and just recently, "Cold Mountain." I have been known to buy tickets at a theater, get some candy, pass out some cash awards, and just leave. I have become rather jaded about movies.

It sure wasn't like that when I was a kid. If I could rake up a dime on a Friday night and get to the Glenway or the Sunset or even the Flop (that's what we called the Overlook), I sat through the whole shebang. Double feature, previews, cartoons, Pathé News, and even the silly musical extras featuring some unknown, at least to me, orchestra.

Sunday afternoons were even better. If you could get out of Benediction early enough, you could make it to the Overlook in time for the matinee. The Sunday matinee had all the features of a weekday night and it had a continuing serial. I never wanted to miss what was happening to "The Whip," Buck Jones, "The Cisco Kid," or Flash Gordon.

I don't really think the movies were better back then. I recently saw "The Missing" at a theater. It is a remake of an old John Wayne film, "The Searchers." Then I watched "The Searchers" on the TV. "The Missing" was far and away the better movie. I stayed for the whole thing.

I think my whole attitude about the movies these days is based on the fact that they are free. You know what they say, "You get what you pay for."

THOSE DIABOLICAL COMPUTERS

April 2004

I'm sitting here, trying to think of something to write about, contemplating my computer. Now, that's something to write about, the computer.

I am self-taught on the computer. That's probably why I don't understand many things about computers. For instance, if something is a *default*, that means it is set to work the same way every time. Why is it called a *default*? According to my dictionary, *default* means "failure to do." You would think that they would have called it a *constant*, that would make a little sense.

On my computer, there is a *non-printing* command. If you didn't want to print, why did you put it in the computer in the first place?

Lettering fonts, the style of the lettering you want to use, are another thing that I have problems with. All the various fonts are there, but they all have different names from what printers used to call them.

I truly believe that computer manufacturers employ resident wizards, who put malevolent demons in each computer. One of those demons is sitting inside my computer right now, just waiting until I get to the bottom line of this article, then just before I save it, he will cause the screen to go blank and everything to go away. When and if I do finish writing this and then try to make the margins, justification, and type-styles correct, another demon, I call him "Spoiler," will make everything go *Sproing!* and the copy will fly all over the place. After fooling around for about an hour, getting things back together, I will save these *pithy mots* for posterity and the newsletter. Unless it decides to go to some nether region of my computer's brain where it can never be found again.

Finally, when I eventually get everything properly done and want to shut down my computer, what command do you think I need to use? Yep, if you want to shut down, you press *"START."*

Editor's Note: The opinions expressed in this column probably reflect the opinions of a whole lot of computer users, but do not necessarily reflect those of the Price Hill Historical Society or its members.

THE CURMUDGEON RAMBLES ON AND ON

May 2004

I was going through some old clothes the other day and I came across an old bathing suit. It was bright orange and had that little diving girl embroidered on the side. Even if it would fit, I wouldn't wear it today. I would consider it indecent.

When I was a kid, back in the dark ages, I belonged to several swim teams. I had a lot of bathing suits. This must be the last team suit I had.

The diving girl on the side was the logo of the Jantzen Company and I got to wondering how this company decided to use this particular symbol. I thought, with the swimming season coming up, this might make a good story.

I did some research on the Jantzen Company and all I found was some very sterile information and nothing about the diving girl. Luckily, though, I know a former executive of Jantzen. He told me the history of the diving girl . . .

In 1874, the Portland Knitting Company of Portland, Oregon, was established by John Zehntbauer and his brother. The company had a small retail store and two knitting machines on the second floor. They made knitted caps and gloves for the lumberjacks in the area.

In 1906, Zehntbauer made a knit swim suit and tried it out in the Columbia River. He thought it was great and displayed it in his store window. Unfortunately, nobody knew what it was. So Zehntbauer found a picture in the *National Geographic* of a diving girl wearing a skirted, full-stockinged, ladies' bathing costume. He put the picture in the window with his swim suit. The picture attracted a lot of attention. The company got so many requests for the picture that they had to have some flyers made with it on them. The picture of the diving girl started appearing in the rear windows of automobiles in Portland. She was probably the first pin-up girl.

The swim suits were not as popular as the picture, however, and the Portland Knitting Company found itself in financial difficulties. Zehntbauer approached a local investor named Hinneman who agreed to lend the company money if they would give his ne'er-do-well son, Mitchell, a job. Zehntbauer readily agreed.

Mitchell Hinneman was a little strange and drove the other five employees crazy. In order to get Mitchell out of the hair of the other employees, Mr. Zehntbauer made him national sales manager and sent him, by train, to New York City. The trip took ten days.

He went equipped with several sample swim suits and a bunch of their diving girl flyers, whose costume now was more like the swim suit they manufactured.

Mitchell's first stop in New York was Stern's Department Store on 42nd Street. He arrived at the buyers office, and immediately, with considerable difficulty, pulled a swim suit over his trousers. The buyer watched his gyrations for a few moments and then called a security guard and had him removed. Stern's buyer immediately called Macy's and other New York stores and Hinneman was stopped at the door when he tried to get in to see the other buyers.

He experienced similar situations in Philadelphia and was almost committed as a mental case. He did no better in Washington, DC. The trip was a complete disaster.

He took a bottle to his hotel room and proceeded to get piflicated. In his stupor, he threw all the diving girl flyers out of his hotel window. The next morning he boarded a train for home. When he arrived back in Portland, he was immediately turned around and sent back to Washington, to call on the prestigious department store, Woodward and Lothrup. Apparently the discarded flyers had done their work and people were clamoring for the new bathing suits.

As Hinneman traveled to Washington, he made it a point to throw handfuls of flyers out of the train window at frequent intervals. And this time when Mitchell spoke to the buyers, he was a little more subdued and they readily ordered the swim suits. Sales of the suits boomed. Woodward and Lothrup suggested the diving girl be put on the swim suits.

In 1916, Zehntbauer decided to incorporate the diving girl into a trademark. He had recently received a written complaint on an unrelated matter from one of his employees. He went to the man and told him that he liked his signature and would like to use it as part of his new trademark.

The employee wanted to know, what was in it for him? After a little haggling, he was offered 25 percent of the company. Carl C. Jantzen agreed and the Portland Knitting Company eventually changed its name to the Jantzen Company and Carl Jantzen became a multimillionaire.

A couple of years later, Mitchell Hinneman, because he considered the dispersing of those flyers from the train window as one of the earliest forms of outdoor advertising, became interested in billboards. Because of his interest in this new form of advertising, billboards began to appear all over the country, all featuring the diving girl, rendered by such famous artists as George Petty and McClelland Barclay.

Print ads for Jantzen appeared in 1921 in *Life* and *Vogue*, and in 1923, a cut-out sticker of the diving girl appeared in an issue of *Men's Wear*. These appeared in the windshields of many autos.

During the fifties, the Jantzen Company logo was the third-most recognized trademark in the country, right after Coca-Cola and Frigidaire.

In the conglomerate business word of today, the Jantzen Company is now a part of the Vanity Fair Corporation and the lovely little diving girl has dove her last dive.

THINGS I COULD LIVE WITHOUT

June 2004

Like any good curmudgeon, I am constantly annoyed by certain little things in life. Store clerks that ignore me, people who don't pick up after their dogs, and junk mail are high on my list. Oversize food packages get to me. You buy a huge box of cereal only to realize, when you open it, it is only half full and on top of that, it doesn't fit on the shelf. Cotton in pill bottles annoys me too, I don't even know why.

These and other things are annoyances, but there are some things that need to be abolished for the good of the human race.

The newest trend in food identification are those little stick-on labels on fruits and vegetables. Any fruit or vegetable larger than a grape had a little oval sticker with, I guess, the name of the grower on it. I have never asked, but I doubt if these labels are edible. Taking one off is a chore. Either it takes a half an hour to lift up enough of an edge to roll it off or you wind up just whacking it off with a knife. A lovely ripe vegetable or piece of fruit shouldn't have a hunk cut out of it just to remove a label. Why do they need labels anyway, anyone over four years old knows an apple from a pear, and if you are under four, you probably can't read the label anyway.

Bubble packs, that's another one. You go to a hardware boutique, like Hader's, to buy a couple of hinges. You can no longer just pick what you need out of a bin; no, everything is hung on the wall in neat little packages. Either the package contains more of the item than you want, or not enough, but that's a gripe for another time. You pay for the hinges, probably about twice as much as you thought they would be. Then you get home and get ready to install the hinges. First you have to get them out of the package. The bubble is firmly secured to the backing—I think they use double strength super glue. Nothing will give. You pick up a screwdriver and try to pry the package open. You gouge your hand instead. Grab a pliers, no luck, you only pinch your thumb. If and when you get the package open, your hands are bloody and bent and you are physically unable to install the hinges.

I have other things I could live without, but I seem to have run out of space. I'll tell you about them some other time. One of the things my daughter can live without is an article that doesn't fit in the assigned space. I try to oblige.

ON THE ROAD AGAIN

July 2004

He who does not know History is destined to repeat it.

Joe Knab, a Walnut Hills High School history teacher, now retired, often said that. I don't think the saying originated with him, I believe George Santayana said it first. Whoever originated it, I think it is true. I am interested in history as, I am sure, we all are. After all, this is a Historical Society.

There is more to history than what we read in books. History is all around us and we should stop and look at places and things of historical import.

When I was much younger, I took my family on several trips around the country. The Interstate Highway system was just being developed, so we generally took state routes.

Just driving down those old roads was a history lesson. You might see the cemetery where Nathan Bedford Forrest was buried, and a little later you might find yourself in the town where Light Horse Harry Lee was born, then drive past life-sized replicas of the Parthenon or even Stonehenge. It always took us a little longer to get where we were going, but the history lessons were always worth it.

Now you drive on an expressway at 65 miles an hour while some guy in a '72 Firebird keeps blowing his horn to make you get out of the way. You have very little time to look for historic sites.

Once I spotted a direction sign that said that Proscathaler's Tavern and Forge were at the next exit. I turned off, and after driving 33 miles, I came across a small, weather-beaten old plaque that told me that this was where Proscathaler's Tavern had once stood and that Richard Henry Lee had stopped there on his way to visit Thomas Jefferson. It was in front of a barn that had painted on its roof, "See Rock City."

Last month I was driving through Virginia. I had planned to take State Route 60 from Lexington, Virginia, to Petersburg, Virginia. I took a wrong turn, and rather than let my wife think I had made a mistake, I just stayed on I-64. It would get me where I wanted to go.

We were coming up on an exit to a town where I remembered there was a historic site that my family and I had visited in the past and always enjoyed, so I pulled off.

(continued on next page)

When you drive into a historic town, the first thing you notice is a large sign with an arrow pointing to the Visitors' Center. There is a sign about every block for about 2 miles . . . then, all of a sudden, the arrow is pointing the other way. We had obviously missed the Visitors' Center.

These lovely little southern towns are hard to drive through. Many of the streets are one way and in this town, most of them dead-ended into a blocked-off section called "The Historic District."

"The Historic District" was a couple of blocks of quaint little, gaily painted buildings which housed mostly coffee houses, antique shoppes, and souvenir stores. It looked like an overgrown miniature golf course.

After driving up one-way streets and down others we finally got back to the main drag. Enough, I decided, and headed back to the Interstate. Suddenly my wife said, "There it is!"

Sure enough, right alongside us was a building with a small, light brown sign that said, in 2-inch pale tan letters, "Visitors' Center." In the center a lovely southern lady was quite helpful and told me, "Y'all just take the Interstate three exits west and y'all will find what y'all are looking for."

We thanked the nice lady and got back on the expressway headed east. Maybe we would visit Tom's place next year.

We finally got to Petersburg and on an old state route, we drove past the Old Blandford Church and Appomattox, but we didn't stop. Like ol' Richard Henry Lee as he neared Proscathaler's Tavern, we were looking for a place to lay our weary heads.

The town was full of race car enthusiasts for some big event, so we had a hard time finding a motel room, but finally we did. As I was going to sleep that night I thought of a revision to that old saying that Joe Knab loved . . .

"He who does not know History probably drives the Interstates."

PITHY MOT

Thomas Jefferson is one of my favorite historical people. He was intelligent, inventive, and colorful. He thought that taxation without representation was a bad thing.

He should see what it is like now, with representation.

SCULPTURE ON THE HILL

August 2004

The Price Hill Civic Club is talking about putting pieces of sculpture in various places on the "Hill." What a great idea, and what a marvelous way to add some pizzazz to our distinctive suburb, but it sounds like a pretty expensive undertaking.

I tried to think of a way that it could be done inexpensively and came up with a few ideas. I think we should use the sculptures to honor past residents of Price Hill and that we should try to keep costs down.

For example, we could gather up a bunch of old 78 RPM music records. They shouldn't be hard to come by. We could spray paint them gold and glue them artistically to a telephone pole at Glenway and Grand, to honor Doris Day.

We would need to check with the Cincinnati Reds, but I think we could get a lot of broken bats from them. We could glue them together to form a large pyramid and place it in front of Western Hills High School. It could be called "Pete's Broken Dream."

Over in Kentucky in a junkyard, there is a lot of residue from old buildings torn down in Newport. We could pick up the cornerstone of one of those old buildings and place it at Glenway and Western Hills as "Jerry Springer's Lament."

At the corner of West Eighth and Hermosa, we could put three whiskey barrels on top of each other . . . "The George Remus Memorial."

There are plans to repair the Sixth Street Viaduct. Maybe we could get one of those pillars with a street light on it and put it at West Eighth and Enright to honor Edward Waldvogel.

In Greenville, Ohio, in a storage warehouse, there is a large, mounted statue of "Mad Anthony" Wayne. I think we could get it cheap and put it at Glenway and Overlook in remembrance of the second pastor of St. Teresa.

Finally, on a serious note, we could get another big hunk of one of those Newport buildings, then take the old fire bell that we have at the Society and put it on top, then place it in front of Elder to honor Larry Schmolt for all the good things he has done for Price Hill.

How about it folks, who would like to sign up now for the "Adrian Lippschitz Comes to Price Hill" Committee?

PICK A CARD, ANY CARD!

September 2004

Our government, in a spirit of generosity and good fellowship, has come up with a plan to save us Senior Citizens some money on overpriced and over-publicized prescription drugs . . . The Medicare Drug Program.

I had never personally looked into the program and knew very little or even cared anything about it. I figured the government had come up with it so it must be a boondoggle.

Recently, though, I read an article in the *Washington Post* by Lisa Barrett Mann about her problems with finding the right Medicare drug card for her mother.

As you probably know, there are several, several, several, kinds of Medicare drug cards. Picking the right one, the one that will work best for you, is apparently a daunting task.

Some of the things that Ms. Mann discovered during her search are astounding. For instance:

- Just because the Medicare.gov Web site says a drug isn't covered under a specific discount card plan doesn't mean it really isn't.
- Just because the Medicare.gov Web site says a drug is really covered doesn't mean it necessarily is.
- The prices Medicare.gov cites for medications under a given discount plan don't necessarily correspond to the prices the plan gives out over the phone.
- The prices that a card sponsor gives out over the phone can differ, depending on whom you talk to.
- Whether Medicare.gov says a pharmacy participates in a given plan doesn't seem to bear any relation to the information the plans, or even the pharmacies themselves, have.

If any of this information confuses you, you can try calling 1-800-Medicare. I tried, off and on, for three days and I never talked to a human being.

So, pick a card, any card. Maybe one of the magicians in Washington can wave his wand over it and make it work, or at least pull a rabbit out of your hat. They are pretty good at that.

Editor's Note: The Price Hill Historical Society is a nonpolitical organization and the views in this column do not necessarily reflect the views of the Society.

If Winter Comes . . .

October 2004

The weather during the past summer has been quite unusual. Last summer was rather cool. So cool, that our local swimming pool started selling coffee just to thaw out the patrons.

The woolly worms not only have long, heavy coats, they are wearing mufflers. There has been an unusual number of strange weather occurrences this year. I, personally, was caught in a tornado on the way home from vacation. Florida has been blown away by an exceptional number of hurricanes and, by the time you read this, New Orleans may be under water. I think all these ominous signs predict a long, cold, and nasty winter.

I don't like winter. I don't care if they are harsh or mild, I don't like winter and I expect the next one to be miserable.

I don't think brisk weather is invigorating. The days are shorter and you must bundle up just to stay warm. Icy sidewalks are treacherous and snowmen are inferior sculptures that leave me cold. Winter is full of tedious chores. Before it even begins, you have to winterize your car, hang the storm windows, and make sure your furnace is working. You have to go out and buy salt and you probably need a new snow shovel.

Speaking of snow shovels, just think of all the snow you have moved from one place or another over the past years. Sixteen tons, I'll bet, or even more.

Driving becomes more difficult. Plowing through two feet of snow is never any fun. If the streets are icy, that's even worse. Even if you can negotiate the bad streets, there is always some nut, driving too fast, who skids and blocks the road, or even worse, plows into your car.

I know what you're thinking—why doesn't this guy just move to Florida?

But I told you before, Florida has blown away. Only 170 more days till spring!

WHAT I DID LAST SUMMER ... (AND SPRING ... AND FALL ...)

November 2004

Last April, I was looking for a project to do. Wouldn't it be neat, I thought, if I could collect recipes from the membership and put them all together in a Price Hill Historical Society cookbook? How much trouble could it be to collect recipes, type them into my computer, and then take them to a printer. How much trouble, indeed?

The first thing I did was ask the members to give me recipes. I guess this was fairly successful; I received a number of recipes. Some were nicely typed and easy to decipher, although some of you may have left out an ingredient or two through forgetfulness, I assume. Some of the recipes were written out in longhand, and some of those were hard to translate. Many of them did not have names of the donors on them. One day I found a bunch of recipes pushed under the door. Those were unsigned.

I spent about a month asking friends, relatives, and perfect strangers for recipes. I finally got a good bunch of them together and started organizing them and typing them into the computer. I was very organized. I entered them in specific categories and included the name of the donor and when I had received each recipe. Things were going along quite smoothly, and then ... my computer broke down.

Luckily, I had saved all my work on a disk. I got a new hard drive installed in my computer and I was back in business. I popped the disk in and ... nothing happened. The new disk drive wouldn't read my old disk. I had to start over. I had to type all those recipes back into the computer. At this point I became completely disorganized. I am sure I lost some recipes, and I apologize if yours was one of them.

From this point on it became a nightmare. My newly repaired computer was very cranky. It would start and stop of its own volition, but I persevered. I finally got it into a semi-book form when I decided that I did not like the type style I had chosen. I went back through the whole thing changing the type.

I finally printed out a copy of the book and edited it. I found lots of mistakes and corrected them. I printed the book again and then edited again. More mistakes and typos. I did this four more times and I am sure there are more mistakes, but I don't care.

I was now ready to transfer my files to a type of file the printer could read. Nothing to it. It took me a month, but finally I took it to a printer. Unfortunately, the way I had set up the files was not the way the printer wanted it, so I had to make some adjustments. Like redo it all over again. The printer called me a day or two after I gave him the stuff. Oh no, I thought, something else is wrong. But it turned out that I had just left out a couple of pages. I had the pages in my files and just e-mailed them to him. He is now busily printing our cookbooks (I hope).

I could not get the kind of cover that I really wanted. It was just too expensive, so I had to look at several other ideas and a lot of people had different ideas. I narrowed them down and designed a cover that I think will be attractive and affordable. I got several people form the Society to look it over and they liked it; even the printer approved.

If the book is available when you read this, you will know that I got it finished. Also know, there will be no sequel.

PITHY MOT

I have learned a lot of things in my life and, probably, I've forgotten most of them again. I went to school and learned to read and write, though some of my critics might question the latter. I learned arithmetic and science and history and geography. Geography was a waste of time, because most place names have been changed since I was a boy. But all things considered, I guess I learned a lot in school. But I think I learned a lot more accidentally, just stumbling through life.

I have learned that poetry does not have to rhyme. That one came as a shocker to me. I learned that you should never read the end of a book first. That takes all the fun out of it. Just like in life, you have to plod through it, learning new things, not knowing what's going to happen, simply enjoying it, without knowing how it's going to end.

EMPTY SPACE

December 2004

Did you ever realize how much empty space you buy each month? Neither did I until a couple of months ago. My wife was preparing dinner and opened a can and discovered that it was empty, there was nothing in it. I'm sure that doesn't happen very often, but it got me thinking. Thinking about how much empty space we buy.

The next time you buy a can of coffee notice how much coffee there is, compared to the size of the can. There is always about an inch of empty space.

Potato chips and other snacks come in big plastic bags which are only about three-quarters full. You have purchased a quarter of a bag of empty space.

My wife recently bought a new hair dryer. It came in a box about two feet square. The dryer was tucked into one small compartment, the cord in another, and the instruction book was under the cord. The rest of the space was, just that, space.

Have you ever seen the inside of a computer? There are three or four little do-hickies in there and some wire. The rest of the space is taken up with, you guessed it, space.

What to do with all this empty space?

I, personally, have become a collector. Some people collect beer cans, some little figurines, some even collect Star Wars memorabilia. I collect empty space.

I put up two shelves in the living room and I keep my empty space on them. They are filling up pretty quickly, so I may have to build more shelves.

> HERE IS A LITTLE SPACE YOU CAN START YOUR COLLECTION WITH.

Visitors sometimes ask me about the shelves and when I explain what I use them for they just look at me oddly.

One tip if you would like to become a collector: Don't use the empty space in a bag of charcoal. It's hard to get the little black specks out of it.

HAPPY NEW YEAR

January 2005

I would like to wish all of you a Happy New Year before I slip into my Scrooge mode. I hope your coming year is bright and joyful. That said, let's talk about holiday displays. The stores start decorating for Christmas before we even celebrate Hallowe'en. That's just too early.

Decorating of houses has gotten a bit ridiculous, too. Thousands and thousands of tiny lights are spread over houses and yards. I can only imagine the glee in the eyes of the Japanese and Chinese who manufacture these lights. Imagine the joy at the electric company when these lights go on and the meter starts spinning. Did you know that in Texas, some people pay professional display companies thousands of dollars to decorate their homes? That's true Christmas spirit. The lights don't bother me nearly as much as the blow-up Grinches, snowmen, and red-nosed reindeer. I got to wondering how this decorating frenzy got started. So I did a little research.

You might be surprised to learn that most of the decorations have nothing to do with the birth of Christ. Even the date is arbitrary. Christ is thought to have been born in the fall, but around 400 C.E., the theologians of the western church selected December 25 because it was the date recognized throughout the Roman Empire as the birthday of various pagan gods. I guess they didn't want to add a new date to their overcrowded calendar.

The Christmas tree idea actually started with a custom in ancient Egypt. On the Solstice, those early Egyptians brought green palm leaves into their homes to symbolize life's triumph over death. The Druids, who venerated the spirit of nature by worshiping oak trees, decorated their homes with evergreens and mistletoe to celebrate the Solstice.

The decorated tree can be traced back to the ancient Romans. During their winter festival, they decorated trees with small pieces of shiny metal.

Sixteenth-century folklore credits Martin Luther as being the first to decorate a tree, but an earlier legend says that a German monk in the seventh century decorated a fir tree and used it to explain the Holy Trinity to the barbarians in the area.

Many of the symbols and practices associated with Christmas are of pagan origin: ivy, mistletoe, the yule log, even magical reindeer. Those ancients probably had snowmen too, but alas they have melted away.

The feasting, the caroling, the gift giving, all are pagan. St. Nicholas, a.k.a. Santa Claus, and the manger are probably the only true Christian symbols of the holiday.

I know you can get giant blowups of Santa and there are probably blow-ups of wise men, shepherds, etc., so next year, if you want to use only Christian symbols, put jolly old St. Nick or a creche in your yard.

I'll Just Walk, Thank You

February 2005

According to the newspapers, our country is filling up with old people. By 2008, over thirty percent of the population will be over sixty-five . . . if we live that long. Getting old is natural and inevitable and certainly better than the alternative.

But as we age, our bodies start to deteriorate. Doctors love this. One of their great joys is to send you to specialist after specialist. These specialists poke and prod you in unseemly places, then shake their heads. They never seem to quite figure out what is wrong with you. That doesn't stop them from prescribing pill after pill to keep you from actually coming down with what might have been wrong with you. Pretty soon you start to rattle when you walk, and with the price of prescriptions today, that's an expensive rattle.

As you age, your mind starts to play tricks on you. My mind still thinks that I am sixteen years old. It tells me that I could easily paint the ceiling in the bedroom, but my knees tell me that I can't even climb the ladder. So I hesitate, reason prevails, and I call the painter.

Occasionally, actually more often than that, my sixteen-year-old mind forgets some of the things it has stored away. Like the name of someone I have known for years or the title of the movie I have driven fourteen miles to see.

There's a question that I ponder whenever driving up my street: If we are living so much longer, why is St. Joseph's Cemetery expanding? They have just finished constructing what appears to be a condominium for the deceased, at Covedale and Rapid Run. They have terraced the hill and built wall after wall of niches for the ashes of the dearly departed.

One of the dubious advantages of living in South Price Hill is that I will soon be surrounded by the graveyard. When my time comes, I won't have to hire a hearse, I can just walk over.

_____

Editor's Note: The opinions and views expressed in this column are those of the Curmudgeon and do not necessarily represent the opinions and views of the Society, my doctors, the staff of St. Joseph's, or even of my wife.

"Let Brown Do It"

March 2005

That's the new slogan of United Parcel Service. They want their customers to call them "Brown" now. But I can't imagine why they are trying to foist the name Brown off on us. UPS is one of the most recognized names in the country.

I have been shipping stuff for years and years and I always said, "UPS it," no matter how it was to be shipped. I can't imagine telling someone to Brown my package.

UPS has even made some improvements since I used them so much. They now give every package a computer number so they can track your package to wherever it is. This tracking service is great. You can call them at anytime and they can tell you exactly where your package is. Isn't that great?

I recently had an interesting experience with UPS. Just before the holidays, one of my children was expecting a package that was guaranteed to be delivered before December 23rd. I took a personal interest, because it was a present for me.

As the guaranteed delivery date came and passed, my daughter started to worry and finally called the national office to track it down. She was told that the package was at the Cincinnati office and that she should call there. She called the local office and was told that the package had not arrived yet but that they had tracked it to Indianapolis. Then she called Indianapolis and was told that it had been there but that it had been shipped to Cincinnati days earlier. I was starting to get worried; it was, after all, my present.

She called the local office again and finally they said that it was in Cincinnati and on the truck. We saw the UPS truck in the vicinity several times, but they never stopped at our house.

She called the local office again and was told that delivery was imminent. The package arrived three days later, well after the December 23rd guaranteed date, and well after Christmas.

I understand that the holiday season is the busiest time of the year for shipping, but the shipper sent this package quite early.

I just don't know what the advantage is in knowing where the package is and that it is on a truck somewhere. So what? The important thing is when it gets delivered.

Well, maybe they do need a new image and "Brown" may serve them well.

TELEPHONE ETIQUETTE

April 2005

When I was a kid, most families had a telephone and it was a very popular convenience. Telephone etiquette was taught to me in school. We learned a lot of basic good manners, such as:

- If you had a party line, you always hang up immediately if another party is on the line.
- If you are calling someone, always identify yourself immediately.
- When answering the phone, a simple but courteous "Hello" is proper.
- If you call a wrong number, apologize for the inconvenience of your call.
- If you receive a wrong number call, courteously explain that the wrong party has been reached.
- Never raise your voice and never slam down the receiver.
- Always close your call with a courteous salutation.

In those days, the telephone was a warm, friendly instrument, and a godsend in an emergency. Today, telephones have become insidious monsters and there are a lot more phones around. Everyone has at least one and many have several. People carry cell phones around in their purses, on their belts, in their pockets, and some even have them attached permanently to their ears. Telephone courtesy is no longer taught in school or apparently anywhere else.

Have you ever picked up the phone and had someone say, "Who is this?" I have little patience with anyone who does that and generally hang up. (I'm not as courteous as I used to be, either.) Answering machines can be annoying too, especially the cute ones. I find it distasteful when a two-year-old kid's voice tries to tell me to call back.

I'm sure all of you have called a company or utility and listened to a recorded voice tell you to press a series of buttons while you futilely hope you'll eventually reach a real human being. Better still, how about when you let the phone ring 17 times and then a recorded voice says, "Please hold." If you hold, you will hear some elevator music, several recorded messages telling you how important your call is, and then the phone goes dead.

Has someone ever awakened you at 3:00 am with a slurred voice asking to speak to Hortense? When you tell them that they have the wrong number, they shout an expletive and hang up.

Mr. Bell, Mr. Bell, what hath thou wrought!

What's in a Word?

May 2005

The English language is very expressive but rather straight-laced and more or less unchanging. Our American version, on the other hand, is just as expressive, far more colorful, and ever-changing. Our language changes everyday, new words and expressions are added constantly. These new words and expressions are usually in the category of slang or technology. I don't know nothin' about technology, so let's talk about slang.

American slang has always been very colorful. You're "the cat's pajamas," or "the bee's knees." Either expression generally meant that you were a person of high esteem to the generation before mine. Or they might have referred to such a person as "the cat's meow."

In my generation, that same person would have been described as "neat," "super," "groovy," or even "far out." In today's society, that person of high esteem would apparently be referred to as "phat" or "dope."

During World War II, we coined a lot of new words and phrases. We "cut a rug" or "jitterbugged" when we danced. When things were going good, we were "in like Flynn" or "living the life of Riley" and we were always looking for "Kilroy."

Americans have always loved their automobiles and have had special names for them, such as "flivvers," "tin Lizzies," "jalopies," "bucket of bolts," "hot rods," and simply "wheels."

The radio, you remember that thing that used to entertain you without pictures, added words and phrases to our lexicon. "A fine kettle of fish," "Jumping Jehosophat," "my aching back," and "Pshaw" are just a few. Television gave us "meathead," "Where's the beef?" and a whole lot more.

We added a lot of descriptive words to the language: "nifty," "spiffy," "ducky," "wicked," "far out," and one of my favorites, "hunky-dory."

Today's generation has added a lot of new words and new meanings to old ones. You know, "You can't teach old dogs new tricks," so I don't really know what most of these words mean.

I do know that "Phat" means good. To "dis," is to say something bad about someone. "Asallright" and "cool dude" pretty much mean the same as "cat's pajamas." I have no idea of what "Fascheisel"* means, but "Outtahere" means I'm leaving, and I'm "Outtahere."

---

*It is the editor's belief that this term is actually spelled "Fa-shizzle," but she would not stake her orthographic reputation on it.

HAPPY 15TH ANNIVERSARY!

June 2005

This month celebrates the 15th anniversary of the Price Hill Historical Society. We have come a long way in fifteen years. I would like to take time out from my curmudgeonly attitude and say some nice things about the organization and the nice people in it.

Our organization has grown from about 21 members in June 1990 to over 600 individual members. We now own the building that houses our headquarters and we have sponsored a lot of great activities. A lot of people have worked hard to make the organization as successful as it is. I think they deserve some thanks.

First of all, thanks to Debbie Horning, who pretty much got this whole thing going, and also to her husband Ed, for all the help he has given us and especially thanks to them for letting us use their loft in the early days.

Thanks to all the members who come month after month to our meetings. I know they only come for the delicious treats we serve, but it is always nice to see them. On the subject of the treats, thanks to everyone who keeps providing them.

Thanks to some of the people we don't see so much any more, some because they moved away, such as John Pierok, Mike Maio, and Joann Mallory. And thanks to Barb Kock and Karen Hummer, who both did a lot for the Society. Thanks to our active members who haven't lived in Price Hill for years but who share their memories and more with us on a regular basis, such as Phyllis Kline, Dave Hamilton, and many others who send us ideas, stories, memories, crafts, and items for our collection.

All who have served as members of our Board of Directors deserve a thank you, as do Rob Geiger and Tom McGraw for serving as coordinators, following in the footsteps of our first coordinator, Debbie Horning.

Valda Moore, Betty Wagner, along with Flo Sparks, Ida Renner, and Janice Chaney, are among those who actually keep our organization running, coming in on Tuesdays and Thursdays to help out, and they deserve our special gratitude.

Julie Hotchkiss, for all the work she has done on the newsletter, and Tom Lindenschmidt for lining up speakers and all the speakers, both deserve a round of applause.

Our gratitude to everyone who shows up at special "work sessions," especially Bob Moore and his tools, and to Larry Schmolt, Dave Sparks, Tim Renner, and Mary Bazeley who are always around when needed.

I know I missed naming some of you, but special thanks to any of you that I did miss, because I am out of space. Thanks to everyone in the Society for your support and interest and thanks to Price Hill for just being here.

Two Sisters and a Third Cousin, Olé!

July 2005

I used to like to watch television in the evenings. *M*A*S*H, Cheers, Northern Exposure*, all great ways to waste an hour or two. Do you remember *Ben Casey, The Dick Van Dyke Show, Star Trek*, and *Peter Gunn*? All good shows, and I could get them when I only had five or six channels. Now I have 72 channels and I can't find anything worth watching.

All I can find are reality shows, which I hate, or home improvement programs, or talking heads, or reruns of *Law and Order*. I switch channels and switch channels until my wife screams and walks out of the room. Finally I settle down to watch how to eat on $40 a day or how to make a new lamp out of an old cesspool cover.

My wife and I recently spent some time at the beach, and the television in our cottage had 202 regular channels, 19 channels that showed only music videos, and 367 channels that simply played music and showed a still picture of the performer. At last, I thought, I should be able to find something to watch! How wrong I was . . .

There must have been ten reality shows. There was even one in Spanish, I think it was called *Two Sisters and a Third Cousin*. I could be wrong, my Spanish is a little rusty. Six or seven of the programs showed people climbing around on ladders doing strange things with sponges, mops, eggbeaters, and paint. Another showed women making string vests. I can't imagine that they would keep you very warm.

The ever-popular reruns of *Law and Order* were available, day or night, with seven or eight spin-offs of the original program. A lot of channels had folks selling various products for $19.95, and reruns of *The Andy Griffith Show* and *Matlock* are always playing on one station or another, but Andy lives in the neighborhood, so I guess that's all right.

A couple of the stations just showed commercials for various realtors and restaurants in the area. My favorite was a three-bedroom, two-bath oceanfront home for just a little less than a half million dollars. Any oceanfront property down there has a life expectancy of about nine years, then it just washes away.

There was a Weather Channel, but our weather was great, so that didn't hold much interest for us. There was another peculiarity about the TV there at the cottage. You could not pick out a program by punching in the channel number. You had to click up or down all the channels to get to the one you wanted.

I used to like watching television . . .

GRANDMA'S SECRETS

August 2005

Some of the modern products we hear about through advertising are sometimes not as effective as their manufacturers claim. You go out and buy a rug cleaner because it claims to eliminate spots on your rugs with no scrubbing. You spray the spot and let it dry, as directed. Then you wipe away the residue and *voila,* the spot is still there.

I find that over-the-counter cold pills are about as effective as the spot removers. I have concluded that products that make extravagant promises usually don't work at all.

Your grandmother didn't need any of these modern solutions to everyday problems. She had a cure for everything. Do you remember? Chicken soup always made a cold seem better. Honey, lemon, and a little whiskey helped a sore throat. Sucking on a clove eased a toothache, and you put butter on a burn. I recently came across some modern "Grandma Secrets." I don't guarantee any of them, but I'll bet they work as well as those new "miracle" products.

- Drinking two glasses of Gatorade can relieve headache pain almost immediately and without any of the unpleasant side effects caused by traditional "pain relievers."
- Colgate toothpaste makes an excellent salve for burns.
- Altoids peppermints will clear up your stuffed nose.
- Mix 1 tablespoon of horseradish in 1 cup of olive oil. Let the mixture sit for 30 minutes, then apply it as a massage oil, for instant relief for aching muscles.
- Get rid of unsightly toenail fungus by soaking your toes in Listerine mouthwash.
- Smart splinter remover . . . just pour a drop of Elmer's glue over the splinter, let dry, and peel the dried glue off the skin. The splinter sticks to the dried glue and comes right out.
- Cleaning liquid that doubles as bug killer . . . If menacing bees, wasps, hornets, or yellow jackets get in your home and you can't find the insecticide, try a spray of Formula 409. Insects drop to the ground instantly.
- Quaker Oats for fast pain relief . . . It's not for breakfast anymore! Mix 2 cups of Quaker Oats and 1 cup of water in a bowl and warm in the microwave for 1 minute, cool slightly, and apply the mixture to affected area for soothing relief from arthritis pain.
- Coca-Cola cure for rust . . . Forget those expensive rust removers. Just saturate an abrasive sponge with Coca-Cola and scrub the rust stain. The phosphoric acid in the Coke gets the job done.
- Heinz vinegar to heal bruises . . . Soak a cotton ball in white vinegar and apply it to the bruise for 1 hour. The vinegar reduces the blueness and speeds up the healing process.
- To disinfect a cut or broken blister, splash on a few drops of Listerine. It's a powerful antiseptic—it already cured your toe fungus!

As I said, I'm not guaranteeing any of these cures or potions, but I am also not asking you to send me $19.95 plus postage and handling.

THEY ALSO SERVED

September 2005

World War II ended on August 15, sixty years ago in 1945. Recently, we have heard many stories about servicemen and civilians who served our country during that great conflict. But I haven't heard anything about what the Boy Scouts did during that time.

I was a Boy Scout during most of the Second World War. Our Scout troop in Price Hill and many others across the country helped the war effort in many different ways.

Every Saturday, our troop would scour our neighborhood, picking up scrap metal, tin cans, old tools, and even empty toothpaste tubes that the people would put out for us on their front porches.

Once a month we would have a paper drive and use the proceeds to buy toiletries and such. We would then pack up the articles and send them to servicemen overseas.

On Wednesday evenings, we would attend Civilian Defense meetings at the Westwood Town Hall. We Scouts were Civilian Defense Messengers. In case of an emergency, we were expected to go to our assigned posts with our bicycles to assist our Civil Defense Warden and his assistants. In case of a communication breakdown, we were to carry messages to other stations.

Luckily, we were only used during simulated blackouts, but we were ready to serve if there had been an emergency situation. At those C.D. meetings, we learned how to spot enemy airplanes and were taught first aid. Many of us were also taught life-saving techniques in case there was an emergency at the river. And a lot of us learned the use of firearms and practiced our marksmanship, just in case . . .

All those efforts might have been just part of our government's plan to make the civilian population aware of the war effort, but I know I felt I was really helping. I was proud to be a Boy Scout and I am still proud to say that I was, and am, a Boy Scout.

Shattered Boyhood Memories

October 2005

When I was a kid, my family would spend a couple of weeks each summer at Indian Lake. My mom and dad, aunt, uncle, cousin, and I would all go. We rented a big cabin right on the lake, and we swam, fished, and went boating.

When I was about 14 or 15, my dad and I would camp up on Fox Island for a few days a couple of times in the summer. We were usually the only ones camping on the island. We swam, fished, boated, and cooked our food over a campfire.

When I hit 16, I went to the lake with a bunch of guys that I hung out with. We did this every year until most of us went into the service. Sometimes we camped on Fox Island; sometimes we pooled our money and rented a cabin. It was a way to get away from our families and show our independence. Once again, we swam and boated, but we did very little fishing. We drank a little beer as most kids our age did. We visited the amusement park, walked across the bridge to the Dance Hall, and tried (usually to no avail) to pick up girls. We seldom got into any trouble and always had a good time.

After we got out of the service, we went to the Lake a few times, as did a lot of other young people from around here. I ran into Gini, who was staying over near St. Mary of the Lake with a group of her girlfriends. I didn't know, at the time, that she would be my wife someday.

I had a lot of fun and some great adventures at Indian Lake. I haven't been back for at least 50 years, so when my wife suggested that we go there for a couple of days, I thought it was a good idea. On a hot day near the end of July, we went back to the Lake, and it has really changed. After 50 years, what did I expect? The amusement park at Russell's Point is gone, as well as the Dance Hall, but oddly enough, the bridge that went between them is still there. I saw only one of the many restaurants that used to be around there. All the beer stands and souvenir shops are gone. Almost all the space was filled with mobile home parks. The place where you used to take rides on sleek Cris-Craft boats is just boat docks for hundreds and hundreds of various kinds of boats. I saw more boats there than I have ever seen on Martha's Vineyard.

We drove around both sides of the lake, and it was unbelievable how many cabins there were and how close together they were. Every one of them had a couple of small boats in their yards.

Needless to say, I was very disappointed. The land of my many youthful adventures had become a haven for pickup trucks, mobile homes, and . . . boats.

We called, canceled our motel reservation, and drove home.

Time and tide, obviously, wait for no man.

More than You Want to Know About Chili

November 2005

I f I asked you what city was the Chili Capital of the world, you might answer Cincinnati. But that's probably because you are from here. So let's start over:

What is the Chili Capital of the world?

Son of a gun, you were right, it is Cincinnati, but how in the world did that happen?

The "History of Chili" begins in 1890, when DeWitt Clinton Pendery concocted the first known Chili Powder mix, which he called "Chiltomaline." Mr. Pendery traveled by horse-drawn stagecoach from Cincinnati, Ohio, and arrived in Fort Worth, Texas. His Chili Powder mix was a hit, and the savory bean stew known as Tex-Mex Chili became very popular.

I have to wonder what would have happened had Mr. Pendery decided to remain in Cincinnati? Would we have been eating that western-style Chili over spätzle with limburger cheese sprinkled on top? Do you think if that was considered Cincinnati Chili, our city would now have more chili parlors than any known city on the continent?

The chili in the Cincinnati area is not truly "chili," as most of the rest of the world knows it. Cincinnati Chili is unique and quite different from its western cousin. In fact, about the only connections it has

to the western version are the meat, cumin, and chili powder it contains. After that, the recipe takes an interesting twist. Cincinnati Chili was "invented" in 1922, when a Macedonian immigrant named Tom Athanas Kiradjieff settled in Cincinnati with his brother, John. He opened a hot dog stand, which he named "Empress," and sold hot dogs and Greek food. He did a lousy business because, at that time, the large majority of the inhabitants of Cincinnati were of German heritage, and nobody in the area knew anything about Greek food, and they weren't thrilled by it. But Tom was not to be defeated. He took a recipe for a Greek stew, maintained the Mediterranean spices of cinnamon and cloves, added some chili powder, changed some of the other ingredients, and called it Chili.

It proved to be a successful experiment. He also came up with the idea of putting it on a bed of spaghetti and selling his Chili in "ways," which is also unique to the area. Obviously, Mr. Kiradjieff's idea caught on in a big way.

(continued on next page)

There are now many independent chili parlors in our town, plus two large chains, Gold Star and Skyline. Gold Star is the largest—they have more stores and cover a wider area—but Skyline, which was started right here in Price Hill in 1949, by Nicholas Lambrinides and his three sons, is far and away my favorite.

I am sure that Mr. Pendery's horse-and-buggy trip to Texas was long and arduous, but I for one am glad he took it. I simply can't imagine that western chili over spätzle could have possibly been as popular as our beloved Cincinnati Chili.

PITHY MOT

The computer is a devious device, intended to frustrate, thwart, baffle, and foil its operator. Actually, I know that the computer is not, in and of itself, malevolent. It is just a machine. Does it think? I don't know. Does a submarine swim?

I do know that there is a tiny Luddite god, a gremlin if you prefer, in my computer, and I suspect there is one in every computer ever made. It knows when I have finished typing a long paragraph. It flashes up the word WHOOPS! and the screen goes blank. And when it does, my precious copy disappears, of course.

I do know how to make a computer go faster: Throw it out the window.

'TIS THAT TIME OF YEAR

December 2005

ime when all the stores are gaily decorated for Christmas, and have been since shortly after Labor Day. Time for you to dash around buying presents for your kith and kin, thanks to those three wise guys. Does anybody know what Myrrh is?

Time to decorate the tree and deck the halls. To find a Yule log and look for a new recipe for a different kind of dressing.

Time for my "Holiday Season Reflections."

Let me start with those Three Wise Men. They gave Jesus those gifts, but the tradition didn't really start there. No one got into the habit of exchanging elaborate gifts until late in the 1800s. The Santa Claus story, combined with an amazing retailing phenomenon that has grown since the turn of the last century, has made gift giving a central focus of the Christmas tradition.

Santa Claus, the guy who started the tradition of putting us all in debt annually, actually was a real person, but you knew that. According to tradition, he was born in the ancient Lycian seaport city of Patara, and, when young, he traveled to Palestine and Egypt. He became bishop of Myra soon after returning to Lycia. The future Saint Nicholas's reputation for generosity and kindness gave rise to legends of miracles he performed for the poor and unhappy.

Clement Moore wrote a poem called "The Night Before Christmas" in 1822 for his family. It was picked up by a newspaper, then reprinted in magazines, and it spread like wildfire. Moore loosely based his benevolent, jolly elf on Saint Nicholas, and that's how all this gift giving got started.

Many folks object to spelling the big holiday of the year "Xmas." The word for Christ in Greek is Xristos. The use of the shortened form "Xmas" became popular in Europe in the 1500s. It also goes well with the word "Sale." Sign writers especially liked it.

The Catholic Church outlawed mistletoe because it had pagan origins. The Church suggested the use of holly instead. The Christian ban on mistletoe was in effect throughout the Middle Ages. Surprisingly, as late as the twentieth century, there were churches in England that forbade the wearing of mistletoe sprigs.

I wish you all the Happiest of Holidays, and a Joyous New Year.

THE MIAMI-ERIE CANAL

January 2006

The Miami-Erie Canal was built between 1825 and 1845, extending 249 miles from Toledo to Cincinnati, Ohio. The canal had 19 aqueducts, three guard locks, and 103 lift locks. The series of 105 canal locks raised canal boats 395 feet above Lake Erie and 513 feet above the Ohio River at Cincinnati, Ohio. Each canal lock was 90 feet long by 15 feet. The entire canal system was 301.49 miles long and it cost $8,062,680.07.

The expansion of the railroads as a means of transportation caused less and less need for the canal. By the late 1870s, it fell into complete disrepair and was no longer used.

Our city officials are currently planning to rearrange Fountain Square at a cost of a gazillion or so dollars. They think it will revitalize downtown and be a tourist attraction. If they want a tourist attraction, I think they should rebuild the Miami-Erie Canal.

No, not the whole 249 miles, just the stretch that ran along Central Parkway. The old subway track bed still exists along the original route of the canal. The city could put a large reflecting pool with a fountain somewhere around the Mohawk area, and then build the canal along Central Parkway. They wouldn't have to do much digging, the subway is still down there.

The canal itself would only need to be 32 feet wide and about 3 feet deep to accommodate the passage of 10-foot-wide sightseeing flat boats. It would start near the reflecting pool at a lock and flow down Central Parkway to Plum and follow Plum to the Convention Center, where it would flow under a footbridge and drop into a retention basin. Then the water would be pumped back to the reflecting pool and back into the canal.

Along the sides of the canal, there should be wide walkways to accommodate push-carts and stalls and vendors of all kinds with shaded seating areas. There should be several footbridges strategically located along the route. The buildings along this walkway should be designed in old style architecture; many of the existing buildings could be retained and renovated. Music Hall would be on the canal, and Findlay Market could be enlarged and extended one block and it would be on the canal, too.

The buildings could house stores of all kinds as well as restaurants, hotels, and specialty shops. It would become a huge shopping mall. There should be large parking areas behind the buildings to make access readily available and a shuttle bus to take people to various stops along the canal's pathway and to the pristine new Fountain Square.

Sure, the city would have to acquire a lot of property to do this, but the property owners could be offered sections along the canal to build on. If that didn't work, there's always "Eminent Domain." Just take their property away from them. After all, it is for the good of the city.

If our fair city wants a four-star tourist attraction, the new Miami-Erie Canal is the way to go.

Remember, you heard it here first.

FEBRUARY IS THE CRUELEST MONTH

February 2006

April is not the cruelest month, unless you are a shady CEO trying to rectify your personal income tax return.

February, the shortest month, has always had to try harder, and has always come up a couple of days short. In the Roman calendar, it was the last month of the year, as the year originally started in March, but the Roman priests kept sticking a day in here and a day in there and finally ended up with a whole new month. They named this new month January, after the god Janus, and were so proud of it they decided that it should be the first month of the year.

February was named for Februus, the god of purification. It has also been called Solmoneth (mud month) and Kalemonath (named for cabbage). So you see, it didn't get no respect.

February is also the cruelest month when it comes to pronunciation. It isn't easy for people to say Feb-ru-ary. The word suffers from dissimulation, which is "the tendency of like sounds becoming unlike when they follow each other closely." People have a tendency to drop the first "r". Dictionaries have actually listed *Feb-yoo-ur-ee* as an alternative pronunciation.

February has some interesting days. Of course, there is Groundhog Day on the second, and Saint Brigid's Day, a national holiday in Ireland, also falls on the second. Saint Brigid was a pagan goddess who was demoted by the early Church. The fourteenth is Saint Valentine's Day and we celebrate the birthdays of both George Washington and Abraham Lincoln in February.

February is a big month for birthdays. A whole lot of famous people were born in this month. My grandson and my grandfather, along with Jimmy Durante, Babe Ruth, and Jules Verne. Clark Gable, Grant Wood, Thomas Edison, Charles Dickens, Charles Lindbergh, and Ronald Reagan all saw their first light of day in this short month.

Such femme fatales as Gypsy Rose Lee, Carmen Miranda, and Yoko Ono, as well as both Zsa Zsa Gabor and her sister Eva, were born in this month. The list goes on and on.

Lord Baden-Powell and his wife, "Lady," both arrived in this world in this month. Chopin, Norman Rockwell, Buster Crabbe, Gertrude Stein, Enrico Caruso, Susan B. Anthony, Jack Benny, James Joyce, and the Old Redhead, Red Barber, celebrated birthdays in February. Dinah Shore and Jimmy Dorsey were born on the 29th of the month, so they just made the list.

February may be considered the cruelest month and the oddest, with the Leap Year thing, but it has certainly provided us with a wealth of famous people.

How Else Are You Going to Learn

March 2006

We get letters and phone calls here at the PHHS all the time from people seeking information about Price Hill. Some folks are looking for old photos of certain areas, and some are looking for family histories or lost relatives or information about old businesses.

Our volunteers diligently try to come up with answers to these queries. They research our files and library. They question older members of the Society. Sometimes they have to go to the Public Library or the Cincinnati Historical Society, but they usually come up with an answer.

The staff seldom allows me to answer any of questions they receive. My laissez-faire attitude—I never let actual history interfere with a good yarn—seems to concern them. But I sometimes get questions about my *Curmudgeon's Corner* column, and I am allowed to answer those.

Last spring, I wrote about slang words, and someone wrote asking me if I remembered when a streetcar was called a "jitney," and why it was called that. I vaguely remember the jitneys, and I remember that a "jitney" was also another name for a nickel. The fare on that early streetcar was a nickel, and that's why fire engines are red.

Another reader asked me why I sometimes put a disclaimer at the end of my column explaining that my views are my own and not necessarily those of the Society. The reader wanted to know if I clashed with other staff members with my view of things. Actually, no one has ever questioned anything I write. I doubt that they read the column at all. I simply use the disclaimer to kill space when my article runs a little short.

One reader questioned my column on Grandma's Secret Recipes. He said that I claimed that "Grandma" suggested taking Gatorade for a headache. He contended that if I was 75 years old, it was improbable that my grandma had ever heard of Gatorade. I didn't say that these were my grandma's secrets, and I also didn't guarantee any results. But—the one that calls for putting Elmer's glue on a splinter really does work.

I have had a lot of requests for my Eggnog recipe. It is pretty complicated, but here it is . . . First, go to United Dairy Farmers and buy their commercial product, then pour it into a punch bowl. Add ½ cup cream sherry per quart of Eggnog. (Omit this step if you want it to be nonalcoholic.) Add a good sprinkling of nutmeg. Finally, throw in a big dollop of French Vanilla ice cream, and then sprinkle with a little more nutmeg and a tablespoon of sherry.

(No need for any kind of a disclaimer this month.)

All Fool's Day

April 2006

Here it is April again, and maybe you have noticed that in past years I have been a little irreverent and have told silly stories that were just basically April Fool's pranks. This year I'm going to tell you a few stories that I have heard about Price Hill and not twist the truth around, just for the fun of it.

The buzz at recent Board meetings has been about the Queen's Towers, the high-rise apartment building overlooking the river. I understand that the property has been sold to a neo-religious group called the Grapes of Wrath Community, or Martha's Miracle Church, or something like that. They plan to tear down the existing building and replace it with a neo-gothic edifice that will contain a 15,000 seat auditorium with plush, velvet kneelers and a 100-foot-high pipe organ. Neither the kneelers nor the pipe organ will be used, they are just for display. There will be an Olympic-size baptismal font in the basement, also for display purposes only. There will be no baptisms performed. They figure if you ain't had it before you joined them, you don't need it.

On the upper floors, there will be a full-size gymnasium with all the modern weight-loss equipment, seven handball courts, and a health food court. Above that there will be several meeting rooms where small groups can discuss business. Happily, the restaurant, Primavista, will remain, but they will only serve haute cuisine Eucharistic bread.

I am also happy to report that the city has decided to go ahead with my idea of rebuilding a section of the Miami-Erie Canal. Work on tearing up Central Parkway begins in mid-June and General Electric has already received contracts to construct the jet-powered canal boats.

On a final note, I would like to update a story I wrote way back in April 2000. I told you about Obadiah Elberon, a war hero, pioneer aviator, and centenarian. At the time I wrote that story Obadiah was 102 years and I am sad to report that he has passed on.

He died on September 20, 2004, exactly 106 years to the day that he was born in that big old stucco house on First Avenue. He was still living, under a cloud, at the nursing home where I first interviewed him. One of the nurses had filed a paternity suit against him. He died peacefully and the suit was dropped. He had requested that his remains should be cremated and his ashes dropped from a plane over Philipps Swimming Pool. He said that all them little black specks would give Miriam Philipps fits. He didn't know that Miriam was past caring.

REFLECTIONS ON "HERITAGE ON THE HILL"

May 2006

Recently I spent an afternoon going through back issues of our newsletter. I started with the December issue in 1999 and worked my way up to December 2005. That's five years, worth, and with 12 issues a year, that's 60 issues. I didn't read every article, but I read parts of all of them. We do a good job with our little newsletter.

We have had good editors in the past and are fortunate to have a good group taking care of business at the present—they've been at it now for a year. They are all to be congratulated on jobs well done. There have been some great articles and stories in our "paper," from a diverse group of authors. They too deserve congratulations.

My column seems to have appeared in every issue except one. I don't remember why I missed that issue, but there must have been a reason.

As I looked at the old *Curmudgeon* columns, I noticed that I have a few pet peeves that seemed to appear over and over: Bad drivers, orange barrels, television commercials for prescription drugs, George W. Bush, and the sloppy use of the English language seem to have annoyed me most. I apologize to any stop sign runners, construction workers, drug salesmen, Republicans, or English 101 drop-outs that I might have offended. I only write for fun and I don't mean to be nasty, but I am required to be a curmudgeon and sometimes, not often, that requires an effort.

I notice that I really like old-time radio, Bob Hope, World War Two songs, April Fool's pranks, and the snacks we have at our meetings. But what's not to like about those things?

Our newsletter is great, with the possible exception of the *Curmudgeon's* column, but I have often thought we should add a cartoon occasionally. My efforts in this category have been feeble at best. Why doesn't somebody out there (hint to my grandsons) submit ideas for topical cartoons? They don't have to be great, and I can fix them up a little.

We really need a cartoon every once in awhile, so I don't have to write such long articles.

50 YEARS OF MARRIED LIFE

June 2006

My wife and I recently celebrated our fiftieth wedding anniversary. Fifty years, that's a long time. Marriage is not just a word, it's a sentence. A life sentence.

It's not a bit unusual for a newly married man to look happy, but after fifty years . . . I can still smile.

I'm sure that none of you old geezers need any advice on a happy marriage but for the few younger members, I have a bit of advice:

- You should always marry a pretty woman (I did) in case you need some other guy to take her off your hands. (I didn't need to.)
- Always tell people that you are in total control, but never say that in front of your wife.
- Don't marry for money, it's cheaper to borrow it.
- Never swear at your wife when other ladies are present.
- Convince your wife, early on, that she would look chubby in a fur coat.
- A happy marriage is one of give and take. The husband gives and the wife takes.
- They say, in China, a man doesn't know his wife until he marries her. Well, it ain't just in China.
- True love is blind, but marriage is an eye-opener.
- All men are born free and equal and then they get married.
- And don't bother to buy an expensive set of encyclopedias after you wed. You will find that your wife knows everything.

That's enough silliness, but I do have one serious piece of advice . . . If you want to stay married for fifty years, be sure your wife is your best friend. In the end, that's what will really keep you together.

Take my wife . . . Please.

But seriously, folks, my marriage is living proof that my wife can take a joke, I hope. If and when she reads this column, I hope she will remember the advice an older friend gave her on our wedding day: "Honey, keep your sense of humor."

Editor's Note: This column does not necessarily express the opinions of the Society or any of its membership. They are the views of the author only, and only his until his wife gets a hold of him.

SHAME ON YOU, LEONARDO

July 2006

The summer movie, "The Da Vinci Code," has caused quite a stir. Many people of various religions are up in arms because it depicts clandestine societies that either advocate the overthrow of religion entirely or, through lying, stealing, and killing, are trying to keep their theology pure.

A fifteenth-century painter, who through the symbolism in his paintings, apparently tore apart the essence of Christianity: The Holy Grail wasn't a cup at all and . . . Jesus Christ was married.

"Holy Mackerel!" Christianity, after having survived for 2000 years, is doomed.

I read the book, but I haven't seen the movie. I probably will, because I enjoyed the book. I did notice on the flyleaf that it said it was a work of fiction. Fiction—that means it ain't true. It's all made up, just a story. Whether Leonardo filled his paintings with catoistic symbolism and was the leader of the Illuminati, or if Robin Hood was a great marksman with a bow and arrow, it just doesn't matter. They are stories, fiction, made-up tales.

Dan Brown's thriller is an ingenious mixture of paranoid thriller, art history lesson, chase story, religious symbology lecture, and anti-clerical screed, and nowhere does it say that any of it is true.

Whenever there is a controversy like this over a movie, the people who gain from it are the people who made the movie. The free advertising value is enormous. Every time someone decries the movie from the pulpit, a few more people decide they have to go see it.

It's always a bad idea to tell people they shouldn't do something. Remember the League of Decency posters they used to put in the back of church? The kids of my day used to check it every Sunday, so they could decide which of the movies listed they wanted to see. So let's calm down. See the movie or not, but if you accept it as a fictional story, I don't think it will drive you away from church.

I remember another movie, from a long time ago. It was called "The Shoes of the Fisherman," and Anthony Quinn played the Pope. I don't remember any controversy over that one. In the final scene, he gave away all the Church's money and treasures to help the poor. Talk about fiction.

The views expressed in this column are strictly those of the author and in no way imply that they are those of the members of the Society, the movie-making industry, or Christianity as a whole. They also do not represent the views of Sister Mary Theresa and Monsignor William Anthony, God rest their souls.

A Price Hill Landmark Still Paddlin' Along

August 2006

Our Incline is long gone, the Peter Neff mansion was demolished, and the Robert Moore house overlooking the city from Mt. Hope Road probably won't last much longer, but our old swimmin' hole, Philipps', is still around.

Philipps' Swimming Pool opened around 1930 and, except for a couple of weeks in 1938, it has been operating every summer ever since. The place had a big fire in 1938 and was forced to close, but only for about two weeks.

The pool was built, owned, and operated by the Philipps family, and I think that somewhere in a back issue of our newsletter there is a brief history of the pool, so I won't go into that. Instead, as I was laying in a lawn chair out there the other day, soaking up a few rays, I decided that I would write about my feelings for the place.

I got my first season pass for the pool in 1935, and on my first visit, Frank Philipps grabbed me and another kid and taught us how to swim in a couple of hours. For the next ten years he saw to it that we continued to improve. That other kid and I have swum for innumerable swim teams and practiced in a whole lot of different swimming pools, but it was Frank Philipps and several other life guards at Philipps who honed our skills.

Thousands of kids must have learned to swim at the pool. Just this morning, as I sat in the sun, I saw all the tiny kids getting their first lessons in the pool. Are there going to be any champions in that group? Philipps' has had some, you know. Frank Philipps and his sister were long-distance champions back in the early thirties. Bobby Fagin, Johnnie Betuchis, Roy Legaly, that other guy, Tom Trame, and others have won state and national acclaim. Even I was a fairly proficient competitor, but my biggest claim to fame is longevity. I have been going to Philipps' for seventy-one years. When I was in Japan, Miriam Philipps sent me season passes every year, even if she knew I couldn't use them—or maybe because she knew I wouldn't be able to use them.

The Philipps family operated the pool for many years until Miriam Philipps died. Then Don Schmidt took over and operated it as a swim club for many more years. A few years ago, Zeek Childers and Denise Driehaus took over at Philipps. They have made improvements, but have kept it the sparkling-clean, fun-filled, family-friendly place that it has always been.

If you happened to see me out there this morning, that lady sitting next to me in the sun is my wife, I met her well over fifty years ago right up there by the deep end. Philipps' Swimming Pool and I started out about the same year. I sincerely hope it outlasts me.

WHAT HATH GOD WROUGHT!

September 2006

That's the first message sent by Samuel Morse over the newly developed telegraph. The telegraph was the forerunner of radio, and I have been thinking about radio all month. That's because I'm preparing a slide show and talk to give at a Radio Operators' meeting, and I recently saw a good movie, "A Prairie Home Companion," which is all about a radio program. I also attended a play at NKU's summer theater called "The 1940s Radio Hour." On top of that, a local radio station has started playing old radio shows.

Those old radio shows always bring back fond memories. I remember sitting on the floor in front of a big wooden box with cloth-covered holes in it and a big green eye right in its center, listening to the adventures of Tom Mix, Jack Armstrong, Tailspin Tommy, Don Winslow, The Hermit's Cave, Mr. Keene, the Lone Ranger, and on and on and on . . . The "real" soap operas in the afternoons, the variety shows in the evening, and the big bands coming to you from the Astoria Ballroom high atop the Hotel Aster in midtown Manhattan. Do you think that orchestra was playing in a fancy ballroom, or were they playing in a dingy little basement studio somewhere? It didn't matter, we could see the band all dressed in tuxedos playing in front of beautifully elegant couples dancing away.

Imagination, that's what radio was all about. We believed what we heard and we saw it all in our heads. I could see the Whistler skulking down a dimly lit street, the Lone Ranger shooting the guns out of the bad guys' hands with silver bullets. Come on, so could you.

And the commercials, sure there were those, too, but it seems to me that they were only on at the beginning and end of the shows: "Pepsi Cola is the drink for you!" "I'm Conchita Banana and I'm here to say . . . " "99/100 percent pure—it floats!"

Today we sit around watching shows on television about people racing each other around the world or jumping off high platforms into a lake, trying to catch eels in their teeth. Maybe you watch the one with all the young singers who try so hard, only to be rudely insulted by one of the dim-witted judges. All those channels and nothing to watch . . . unless you are into remodeling an already beautiful old mansion or you want to learn how to knit a toilet paper cover-up.

Worse than all the stupid shows are the stupid commercials, and the same ones play over and over and over. The ones that bother me the most are the pharmaceutical ads that promote prescription drugs, but you knew that. Second to those are the ones that think you know what they are selling. Like the one with all the colorful acrobats forming spectacular pyramids and they show a bull's-eye??

In another one, they show athletes jumping all over and then you see a foot or a lightning bolt or something, I have no idea what that one is selling. Then there's the one that keeps repeating—"just rub it on your forehead, just rub it on your forehead, just rub it on your forehead." Is it for giving yourself a greasy forehead or what? I don't think they ever tell you what it does. Oh, give me back Stella Dallas and Front Page Farrell!

PITHY MOT

When I write these monthly columns, I always worry a little bit about infringing on someone else's ideas. But I have finally come up with a formula:

> If you copy from a single source,
> that's plagiarism.
> If you copy from a lot of places ...
> that's research!

DING, DONG, GONE WENT THE TROLLEY!

October 2006

f you're old enough to remember streetcars, did you like them? I kind of did. They were slow, fairly quiet, except for an occasional clang, clang, and they didn't use any gasoline.

Unfortunately, Cincinnati has a great facility for screwing up its landmarks and keepsakes—no more streetcars, inclines, fancy theaters, or subways. That last one never even got finished. It's a pity that we couldn't have kept some of those things around.

But, getting back to the streetcars or electric trolleys. Progress just made them obsolete, or did it? Maybe progress had a little help. In 1922, according to GM's own files, Alfred P. Sloan, Jr., the MIT-trained genius behind General Motors, wanted to expand auto sales and maximize profits by eliminating streetcars. Sloan established a special unit within the corporation which was charged, among other things, with the task of replacing America's electric railways with cars, trucks, and buses.

By threatening to divert lucrative automobile freight to rival carriers, they persuaded the railroad to convert its electric street cars to motor buses—slow, cramped, foul-smelling vehicles whose inferior performance invariable led riders to purchase automobiles. They also offered banks with rail clients millions in additional deposits if they persuaded those clients to convert to motor vehicles.

With a pack of notorious mobsters, GM helped purchase and scrap the street railways. Where rail systems were publicly owned and could not be bought, the public officials instead, according to FBI files, were provided complimentary Cadillacs if they converted to buses.

To be fair, GM wasn't the only one involved in this conspiracy. Several major oil companies, local auto dealers, and tire manufacturers apparently also had a hand in the demise of the trolley.

But at a time when our venerated leader, George W. Bush, is ringing his hands about the vast amount of oil we consume and trying to come up with electric automobiles, maybe we should think about bringing back the streetcars.

Editor's Note: Research for this article came from The New Electric Railway Journal, *Autumn 1995, and does not necessarily express the views of anyone except the Old Curmudgeon.*

LIFE IN THE 1500s

November 2006

I have to thank my wife, Gini, for sending me this story. I thought it was interesting enough to pass along and besides it saved me from having to write a column this month.

The next time you are washing your hands and complain because the water temperature isn't just how you like it, think about how things used to be. Here are some facts about the 1500s:

Most people got married in June because they took their yearly bath in May, and still smelled pretty good by June. However, they were starting to smell, so brides carried a bouquet of flowers to hide the body odor. Hence the custom today of carrying a bouquet when getting married. Baths consisted of a big tub filled with hot water. The man of the house had the privilege of the nice clean water, then all the other sons and men, then the women, and finally the children, last of all the babies. By then the water was so dirty you could actually lose someone in it. Hence the saying, "Don't throw the baby out with the bath water."

Houses had thatched roofs, thick straw piled high, with no wood underneath. It was the only place for animals to get warm, so all the cats and other small animals (mice, bugs) lived in the roof. When it rained it became slippery and sometimes the animals would slip and off the roof. Hence the saying, "It's raining cats and dogs."

There was nothing to stop things from falling into the house. This posed a real problem in the bedroom, where bugs and other droppings could mess up your nice clean bed. Hence, a bed with big posts and a sheet hung over the top afforded some protection. That's how canopy beds came into existence.

The floor was dirt. Only the wealthy had something other than dirt. Hence the saying, "dirt poor." The wealthy had slate floors that would get slippery in the winter when wet, so they spread thresh (straw) on floor to help keep their footing. As the winter wore on, they added more thresh, until when you opened the door it would all start slipping outside. A piece of wood was placed in the entrance way to keep the thresh in. Hence we still walk over the "thresh hold" to enter a house.

In those old days, they cooked in the kitchen with a big kettle that always hung over the fire. Every day they lit the fire and added things to the pot. They ate mostly vegetables and did not get much meat. They would eat the stew for dinner, leaving leftovers in the pot to get cold overnight and then start over the next day. Sometimes stew had food in it that had been there for quite a while. Hence the rhyme, "Peas porridge hot, peas porridge cold, peas porridge in the pot, nine days old."

Sometimes they could obtain pork, which made them feel quite special. When visitors came over, they would hang up their bacon to show off. It was a sign of wealth that a man could "bring home the bacon."

(continued on next page)

They would cut off a little to share with guests and would all sit around and hence the saying, "chew the fat." Those with money had plates made of pewter. Food with high acid content caused some of the lead to leach onto the food, causing lead poisoning death. This happened most often with tomatoes, so for the next 400 years or so, tomatoes were considered poisonous.

Bread was divided according to status. Workers got the burnt bottom of the loaf, the family got the middle, and guests got the top, or hence "upper crust."

Lead cups were used to drink ale or whisky. The combination would sometimes knock the imbibers out for a couple of days. Someone walking along the road would take them for dead and prepare them for burial. They were laid out on the kitchen table for a couple of days and the family would gather around and eat and drink and wait and see if they would wake up. Hence the custom of holding a "wake."

England is old and small, and the local folks started running out of places to bury people. So they would dig up coffins and would take the bones to a "bone-house" and reuse the grave. When reopening these coffins, 1 out of 25 coffins were found to have scratch marks on the inside and they realized they had been burying people alive. So they would tie a string on the wrist of the corpse, lead it through the coffin and up through the ground, and tie it to a bell. Someone would have to sit out in the graveyard all night (hence the "graveyard shift") to listen for the bell; thus, someone could be "saved by the bell" or was considered a "dead ringer."

And that's the truth . . . Now, whoever said that history was boring!

POLITICS AS USUAL?

December 2006

The Price Hill Historical Society is a non-political organization. I appreciate that and try to abide by it but . . . The political campaigns leading up to our last election that we have seen are an abomination. I waited until after the elections to write this, but if everything I heard on the commercials is true, we are in trouble.

No matter who won, we now have a dirty, double-dealing, embezzling, war-mongering, sexually perverted crook in office. Have you ever seen anything like the ads and commercials we were subjected to during this past campaign?

The only thing any of the politicians (on both sides) talked about was how dreadful their opponents were. How they didn't show up to vote when called upon to do so. How they wasted, or even worse, embezzled our tax money. How they took worldwide trips and vacations paid for by self-interest lobbyists. How each in their own way would raise our taxes and escalate the war.

Everything that was said may well be true. I personally think that there are a lot of problems with the people we choose to run our government, but I hope and pray that the ones who won are not as bad as they were painted.

What ever happened to those nice commercials that showed a candidate standing in front of a nice, modestly priced home with his wife and four nice children telling what a nice guy he was and he would like it very much if we voted for him? I do think Judge Dinkelacker did run one like that. I hope he won, just because he didn't knock anybody. His was the only positive ad I saw.

I think that all politicians are possibly a little shady, it goes with the territory, but I didn't need to have my ears pounded about how awful they are, especially when it is their opponent probably lying through his teeth about them.

I have been voting since I was 21 and I don't think I ever missed an election in all that time, but this year I came close to not voting at all. I did eventually vote for those I considered the least likely crooks. I also voted for Dinkelacker.

Another thing that annoyed me this year was all the phone calls. I must have received over a hundred in the last week alone. George W. and his wife called several times. It was nice to hear from them, but when I asked Mr. Bush to stay the course, he hung up on me. Bill Clinton also called a couple of times. I'm a little worried about ol' Bill. He is obviously working too hard.

The football player Anthony Munoz called to chat, as did Chabot's mother, several of the candidates themselves, and a lot of unidentified people. A little old lady screamed at me that they were going to take our Social Security away from us. She didn't say who "they" were. Elections would be all right if it wasn't for the candidates . . . and the telephone.

This column reflects only the views of the Curmudgeon and not necessarily those of the Society or any of its members.

PVDC (Potentially Vicious Demonic Cellophane)

January 2007

PVDC film, better known as Saran Wrap, Glad Cling Wrap, or Handi-Wrap, is truly the Devil's evil handiwork. Each roll is imbued with the spirit of a malevolent demon. "Just put some Saran Wrap over those leftover tomato slices," my wife tells me, and I cringe. Saran Wrap is my ultimate nemesis. "Nonsense," I tell myself, "I can do this."

I get out the Saran Wrap, I can't find the edge, I run my fingernail around and around until I find it. It doesn't come off in a whole piece. I keep pulling pieces off, trying to get it even. Eventually I get the stuff straightened out and realize that I have about seven feet of shredded plastic behind me, so I try to tear it off from the roll. I line it up with the serrated box lid and pull. The box flies one way and the roll of plastic wrap falls to the floor and unwinds about another four feet. I whack off the eleven feet of now wadded-up plastic wrap with a butcher knife and throw the wad away.

Now I have an edge, although a little hacked up, to hang on to. So I start pulling off some plastic wrap. I am pulling from the middle so the sides fold back and adhere permanently to the underside of the sheet. I try to separate them and soon have another rather sizeable ball of plastic. I carefully cut this off the roll with a scissors, throw the mess away, put the Saran Wrap back in the cupboard, and dump the tomatoes. Once again, I am frustrated by a seemingly benign, almost invisible kitchen aid.

According to history, the Devil did not actually invent plastic wrap. But you can bet he inspired its discovery. In 1933, Ralph Wiley, a lab worker, accidentally (or was he diabolically motivated?) discovered polyvinylidene chloride, or PVDC, as a college student cleaning glassware in a Dow Chemical lab. One day he came across a vial he couldn't scrub clean, obviously demonic intervention. He called the substance "eonite," after an indestructible material in the comic strip "Little Orphan Annie."

Dow researchers made Ralph's eonite into a greasy, dark green, smelly film. The military sprayed it on fighter planes to guard against salty sea spray, and car makers used it for upholstery. Dow later got rid of the green color and the unpleasant odor. After World War II, PVDC was developed into a transparent plastic film approved for food packaging. It was renamed Saran. Saran films are best known in the form of Saran Wrap film, the first cling wrap designed for commercial use (1949) and household use (1953), introduced by the Dow Chemical Company. The insidious Saran Wrap brand plastic film is now marketed by S. C. Johnson.

Saran Wrap demons are obviously prejudiced, as I have seen my wife use the product with ease, while in my hands it becomes a snarling, twisting, uncooperative beast, determined to stick everywhere but where I want it to. I hate plastic wrap, plastic wrap hates me. Long live aluminum foil.

No Complaints

February 2007

It is a beautiful warm day in January as I sit down to write this column. I certainly can't complain about the weather, because this winter has started off very pleasantly. I always complain about traffic, TV commercials, and the lack of proper war songs. I really haven't gotten much mail lately, so there's nothing to write about there.

On a hunch, I looked up some of the laws we live under here in the state of Ohio. Some of these are old and probably not enforced anymore, but they are on the books . . . For example:

- The Ohio driver's education manual states that you must honk the horn whenever you pass another car.
- It is illegal to mistreat anything of great importance.
- Participating in or conducting a duel is prohibited.
- Owners of tigers must notify authorities within one hour if the tiger escapes. (That seems like a good law, actually.)
- In Ohio, if you ignore an orator on Decoration Day to such an extent as to publicly play croquet or pitch horseshoes within one mile of the speaker's stand, you can be fined $25.00.
- In Clinton County, any person who leans against a public building will be subject to fines.
- In Cleveland, it's illegal to catch mice without a hunting license!
- A Columbus law states that it is illegal for stores to sell corn flakes on Sunday.
- In Youngstown, riding on the roof of a taxi cab is not allowed. And you may not run out of gas.
- In some areas of the state, you cannot eat a doughnut and walk backwards on a city street, and it is against the law to roller skate without notifying the police.

Yes, I know that there ought to be a law against wasting a column like this, but I just couldn't think of anything to gripe about. My life must be too good lately. I should go out and eat some worms.

This column does not necessarily reflect the views or opinions of the Price Hill Historical Society, or of any of its members or officers. In truth, it does not even reflect the opinions of its author, the Old Curmudgeon.

SAY CHEESE!

March 2007

The first successful photograph was produced in June or July of 1827. This picture required an exposure of eight hours. By 1829, Louis Daguerre had discovered a way of developing photographic plates, a process which greatly reduced the exposure time from eight hours down to half an hour.

Sir John Herschel is credited with coining the word "photography," a term which he used in a paper he presented to the Royal Society on March 14, 1839. He also coined the terms "negative" and "positive" as they are used in photography, and was the first person to use the term "snapshot."

Through the nineteenth century, photography was a very difficult, time-consuming, and labor-intensive undertaking and was only indulged in by serious, well-trained enthusiasts. But with the arrival of the twentieth century, the amateur shutterbug burst upon the scene because of a camera innovation. Introduced in 1900, the Box Brownie was a small box camera, designed by Frank Brinell and made from jute board and wood. George Eastman manufactured the camera and gave it the name "Brownie." It sold for $1 in the United States.

The Box Brownie was an instant success, and within the first year, over 100,000 had been sold. Everybody owned one and everybody was running around taking pictures. So where are all those pictures now? A lot of them were underexposed, overexposed, poorly posed, or blurry because "somebody moved." And a lot of them got thrown away for many other reasons, but I know there are still some around packed in old boxes, tucked away in closets, or up in the attic. We need those old photos!

I have a scanning system set up at the Society headquarters now. If you bring in your old photos when we are open, we can scan them on the spot and return them to you immediately. If you mail them to us, we will copy them and mail them back.

So, take a look around. They don't have to be from the 1900s. We're looking for stuff from the 1930s, 1940s, 1950s, and even more recent history. Personally, I am looking for any photos of the seven moving picture theaters that were once in Price Hill, drug stores, and other businesses. I would also like a shot of Peggy's Grill. Look around, see what you can find, and stop by to share your old snapshots with us at the PHHS.

UNEXPECTED EXCAVATIONS

April 2007

If you have been to our headquarters or have driven down Warsaw recently, you have probably noticed that the buildings on the south side of the street are gone. Kroger's has finally gotten their act together and started tearing down those old buildings.

The demolition has been almost like an urban archeological dig. Some strange things have been unearthed. For example, up at the western end of the dig, a torn movie poster was found. It advertised "Boston Blackie and the Tea Party," and it was wrapped around two petrified packages of Necco Wafers. A little to the east, an A & P coffee can was found. In it was a wooden disk with printing on it. Although it was hard to read, it seemed to say "Good For One Beer—Haberstumpf's Garden." There was also a can opener marked "P.H.P.& G" and an envelope from Gander Meats, full of little red round things. In about the same area, there were several rusty campaign buttons that read "Dempsey, Dempsey Is the Man."

Down Warsaw, there was found an old Cleo-Cola case filled with Lackmann's beer bottles and nearby, a Prince Albert tobacco can held tokens from the Price Hill Inclined Railroad. Over closer to Kroger's, an old tin bucket was unearthed, printed with the slogan, "A Souvenir of the 1937 Flood." Close to it was a Tom Mix pocket knife and a broken Shirley Temple pitcher.

In the general area, there were many other treasures unearthed: a wooden shoehorn from Marmer's, a bottle of cough syrup marked Dugan's. There was a two-holed bowling ball and two-and-a-half pairs of roller skates. Also a book marked "Return to Warsaw Library April 1, 1913," and a stirrup stamped "CPD-Dist 3." Maybe the most amazing find was an old, termite-eaten, wooden mannequin still wearing a tattered old long-skirted plaid uniform with a crest on the jacket that had the initials "St. V. A." embroidered on it.

If you expect to see any of these items displayed in our Warsaw Avenue museum soon, keep in mind that it is April, and don't hold your breath.

The Second Greatest Show on Earth

May 2007

The medicine show had its origins in the performances put on by traveling charlatans as early as the fourteenth century in Europe. In early America, entrepreneurs calling themselves Doctor or Professor presented their own medicine shows. They were fast-talking con men who claimed that their elixirs and potions would cure any and all ailments, even illnesses that they made up. They were surprisingly successful, probably because there were few doctors and medicines available and because most of those patent medicines contained a large amount of alcohol. One of those early remedies was said to contain snake oil, and those early pharmaceutical representatives became known as "Snake Oil Salesmen."

Some of those entrepreneurs were so successful that their products gained national attention. Lydia E. Pinkham's vegetable compound, Fletcher's Castoria, and even Angostura bitters started out in medicine shows, and the most successful medicine show ever promoted another magic elixir, Hadacol.

Many of those early snake oil companies are still around. You can still find Bromo-Seltzer, Carter's Little Liver Pills (currently sold as Carter's Little Pills), Chlorodyne, Doan's Pills, Fletcher's Castoria, Geritol, Goody's Powder, Lobeila Cough Syrup, Luden's Throat Drops, Phillips' Milk of Magnesia, Lydia E. Pinkham's Vegetable Compound, Smith Brothers Throat Drops, Vicks VapoRub, 66 Cold Medicine, Absorbine Jr. . . . and a lot more.

Others started giant pharmaceutical empires and they now use the television like they used to use radio—and before that they used the wagon shows. Their pitch is slicker and more refined, but their motto is still the same, "Whatever you've got, our elixir will cure it." One of those big companies just recently pulled the old Listerine trick. They had a pill that they made to help Parkinson's patients that didn't work too well. So, they invented a disease that it would help, and that's how restless leg syndrome came to be.

As always, the views expressed here are those of the Old Curmudgeon, and not necessarily those of anyone else.

BUTTON, BUTTON, WHO'S GOT THE BUTTON

June 2007

I mentioned in one of my past columns that I was a collector of the empty space that comes in the packages I buy. It is an interesting hobby, and I recently discovered that I collect something else.

I collect buttons. I just got to thinking about buttons, so I decided to see how many buttons I actually had. By my count, I currently own 1,522 buttons. Does that sound unreasonable? Shucks, there are 577 buttons on my shirts alone.

There are 68 buttons on my phones, not counting the cell phone, which has 18. There are 345 on my computers, 11 on the TVs, and 112 on the three remote controllers. My world is inundated with buttons. Look around you—you too are surrounded.

There are those nice round buttons that keep our clothes from falling off of us, and they have been have been known to exist as far back as the Bronze Age, when they were worn as ornamentation. Primitive man used thorn and sinew to hold clothing together. The Egyptians used cloth ties and broaches or buckles to hold their clothes together. The Greeks and Romans are thought to have worn buttons to actually fasten clothes.

The push button didn't really get a start until electricity was discovered, but then just think of it, pushing a button in the wall to bring the sun indoors was magical. Radio was probably the first push-button home entertainment device and look at them now. We live in a push-button world, just as a 1942 edition of *Popular Mechanics* predicted.

There are at least 62 buttons in our kitchen, even two inside the refrigerator that turn on and off the lights. I didn't count the buttons on our washer, dryer, or vacuum cleaner, because my wife won't let me touch them for fear I'll break them.

My car has 52 buttons, and that's not counting the horn. So I guess you can see that my collection of buttons is extensive, and so is yours. You too, are a button collector, whether you realize it or not.

If a coin collector is a "Numismatist," we should probably consider ourselves "Compescormists."

ROCKY MOUNTAIN HIGH

July 2007

I've had a lot of good ideas in my life. Unfortunately, none of them paid off. For example, I came up with a marvelous idea for a kids' toy. It was called "STICK." It was about 32 inches long and about 1 inch in diameter. It came in a long plastic sleeve that served as a storage bag. A kid could throw it, jump over it, twirl it, whack with it, and balance it—it was a universal toy, but someone told me it was stupid, so I didn't market it.

Another great idea was the miniature sandbox, a shallow bowl filled with sand, some pebbles, and a little rake. One could rake little designs in the stand and highlight them with pebbles. Once again, I was told it was dumb. Later someone else came up with the same idea.

Then there was the "PRETZYMUG." It was a container made out of a pretzel. You put your beer in it and then you drank a little, snacked a little. Once again, I was told it was a stupid idea. Go to Panera's and see how they serve their soup.

Of all the hair-brained ideas I've had, nothing compares with the idea of putting water in bottles and selling it. There's at least one sink in every house, most buildings have water fountains, and you can always find a bubbler in a park. What do you think friends said about that idea when Mr. Perrier thought it up? But he persisted; the rest is history.

So I've come up with the big one—bottled air. I know you can get portable oxygen. But this would be air. You take the lid off a bottle, then put it back on and you have ten ounces of air. And it comes in several flavors, including SEABREEZE™, bottled on the shores of old Nantucket, ROCKY MOUNTAIN HIGH™, from the peaks of the Rockies, and KENTUCKY BLUE™, with the tangy smell of stables on a sunny morning.

Now, this idea has some real merit. It just needs more study.

(To Be Continued)

Bottled Air!

August 2007

As promised, more about bottled air this month. I thought it deserved another column. Just imagine, you are in Hawaii, visiting a live volcano. The air is thick, and it smells of sulphur. You are quite uncomfortable. Pull that bottle out of your back pocket pop, the cap, breathe deeply. Ahhh! Fresh air!

Or what if, God forbid, there was a fire with heavy smoke—you're trapped, but then you whip out a bottle of handy-dandy bottle air and breathe easy. Bottled air may be the super product of the future. It would be inexpensive to produce. A premium of a penny apiece could be offered for the return of empty air bottles. Kids and homeless persons would jump at this idea of making a little spending money, and litter patrols would be thrilled to see these bottles disappear from the roadsides. A new label could be pasted over the bottle, and of course the product to put in the bottle can be found anywhere. Just tell the customer that it comes from exotic places—that's marketing.

Air is light, so shipping charges would be negligible. The biggest cost, as I see it, would be new caps. I don't see any way around that. Including a massive advertising campaign, costs would be about five and a half cents a bottle. If a bottle sold for $1.25, that would leave a profit, after commission to the purveyor, of about 66 percent, or about 82 cents a bottle; not bad for very little effort. With such clever names as the aforementioned "Rocky Mountain High"™, "Seabreeze"™, "Kentucky Blue"™, and new ones, including "Bahama Zephyr"™, "Tradewinds"™, and "Wispy"™, success would be inevitable. For the international market, the product could be called "Eau de Paree"™, "Kuku Ureshii"™, and "London Derriere"™.

I have been told, time and time again, that my ideas are dumb, so I never give them a fair trial. This one is different. With the state of our world today, war and pestilence and global warming, the time is ripe for bottled air—it will become the opiate of the masses. "Air Vendors" will magically appear at every outdoor event. There will be kiosks along major boulevards and drive-ins with names like Airasis and Pater Nostril.

Imagine a loving couple in a canoe, serenely drifting along a fetid, smelly river, sharing a bottle of "Kentucky Blue"™. You could be stuck in a traffic jam, fumes from all the idling engines starting to build up. It is becoming intolerable . . . just look in your glove compartment, because bottled air doesn't need refrigeration. Grab that bottle, pop the top—sweet relief.

This is it—this is the big one. Don't miss your chance to get in on the ground floor. Now is the time to invest in stock in AIR AMERICA AND BEYOND LIMITED®.

A Not So Amusing Column

September 2007

I always try, in my own feeble way, to put some humor into my column. This one will be different. The other night, I was watching the national news and they featured "Someone Making a Difference," a man who was looking for buglers to play "Taps" at military funerals. It seems that at some funerals, "Taps" is played by a recording because there are not enough buglers to go around. The current war has put a strain on the buglers of our country.

Why does our country get involved in these stupid little wars? For oil? That's what I have been told about Iraq. Then did we go to Grenada because we were short of Grenadine? Korea, Vietnam, what were we after in those places? Or is it our government just trying to control the population? Even I don't believe that. American lives are being lost every day and for what? So huge businesses can make huge profits or simply steal our—the taxpayers'—money?

As far as I can see, none of our wars since World War II have had a clear victory. Actually, they looked a lot like defeats to me, and to what end? They probably made changes in the world, but none that I can see.

Almost every generation gets its own little war. Mine was Korea. I was in the Air Force, and liked it. I was in the Far East, and I liked that too. The only time I was in any kind of danger was when a mob of Communists threw beer cans at me. Even then I thought it was a stupid war, or, excuse me, that was a "Police Action," wasn't it?

Going to war interrupts lives at best and at worst it can leave someone crippled or dead. War seems stupid to me. Why don't the people I elect to rule the country see it my way, at least once in a while?

This is the second draft of this column that I wrote tonight. I showed the first one to my wife and she told me I couldn't put something like it in our little newsletter. I took members of our past and present government to task for what I considered to be their lies, deceit, and false claims that led the way to hostilities. My wife said that I didn't know, for sure, what I was talking about. It's true, I don't know anything about why we are spending billions and billions of dollars on faulty body armor and other equipment. Maybe there is a good reason why we have to put the flower of our youth in harm's way.

Maybe she is right, I probably don't know what I'm talking about, but what has become of the American Way? Maybe we just need a new crop of buglers.

Editor's Note: The views expressed here are those of the Curmudgeon and do not necessarily reflect the views of the Society or any of its members.

ONE MORE BUMP IN THE NIGHT

October 2007

It was a nice summer. A little hot for a while, but I like it hot, a lot better than I like the cold, and the cold is coming. By the end of the month, we will be bundling up to ward off the chill.

It seems to me that the end of this month is always when you have to start wearing heavy coats. On October 31, all those little ghoulies and ghosties and night bumps usually have to cover up their cute costumes with a coat or slicker or something.

Those little urchins in their K-Mart classic costumes probably don't realize it, but they are keeping remnants of the distant past alive. Romans observed the holiday of Feralia, intended to give rest and peace to the departed. The Druidic fire festival called Samhain (*sow' ain*), the Feast of the Dead, was celebrated by the Celts throughout Scotland, Wales, and Ireland. These festivals were observed at the end of harvest time, around the first of November.

Later, the newly arrived Christians were unable to get the people to stop celebrating those pagan holidays, so they declared the day one of their holy days. The Church fathers simply sprinkled a little holy water on it and gave it a new name, "All Saints' Day."

The day before this holy day was the "Sanctified Eve" or "Hallow E'en," (in Old English the word hallow meant "sanctify"), and the Church called it All Souls' Day—October 31.

But you knew all that. "Greeting card holidays," that's what I call them—Christmas, Mothers' Day and Fathers' Day, Easter, Valentine's Day, Hallowe'en, et al.—they have just become too commercial. The card, candy, flower, and gift companies are way too greedy. And the stores all start displaying their wares for one holiday before the last one has even arrived. It's ridiculous.

Remember when you were a kid? You carved your own pumpkin, you didn't go out and buy a plastic one. You or your mother probably made you a costume. You went out begging, and you didn't go out during specified hours. And if someone gave you a nickel candy bar, you told everybody where it came from. Some people decorated a little, but only close to the big day, and they didn't put giant blow-up figures in their yard—figures that are quickly out of air, lying in the yards deflated. I hate those blow-up figures!

A NOBLE BIRD INDEED

November 2007

As one of the few Druids in the Price Hill Historical Society, I like to go back and show how our modern holidays have their origins in the prehistory days of the pagans. You've probably noticed that in previous columns.

I have done it with Easter, Hallowe'en, and Christmas, so I thought I would look into the Thanksgiving origins and, much to my dismay, I discovered that Thanksgiving Day is pretty much just what we thought. It's an all-American holiday started by those early Pilgrims in 1621, to commemorate the first harvest reaped by the Plymouth Company after a harsh winter.

It wasn't an original idea, of course. The custom of celebrating a successful harvest goes way back and is virtually universal. For as long as people have been planting and gathering food, I suspect there probably has been some form of Harvest Festival or, at the very least, a really great dinner when the harvest was in.

The early pagans in England celebrated at least three harvest festivals, which were called Ingathering, Inning, and Kern (possibly a corruption of the word corn), all festivals held to celebrate the end of the harvest season.

The Algonquin tribes at the time of the Pilgrims held six harvest festivals during the year. So, even if it wasn't an original idea, our forefathers started an original holiday. At that first celebration of a good harvest, Governor William Bradford proclaimed it to be a day of thanksgiving. The colonists celebrated it as a traditional English harvest feast, to which they invited the local Wampanoag Indians. The governor sent men out after wild ducks and geese. Turkey was probably not a part of that original feast; however, it is certain that they had venison.

George Washington proclaimed a national day of Thanksgiving in 1789, but it was Sarah Josepha Hale, a magazine editor, whose efforts in the mid-eighteenth century eventually led to the holiday we recognize today as Thanksgiving. At Hale's urging, President Abraham Lincoln proclaimed the last Thursday in November as a national day of Thanksgiving to be celebrated every year. The date was changed a couple of times, most recently by Franklin Roosevelt, who moved it up one week, to the next-to-last Thursday, in order to create a longer Christmas shopping season. Public uproar against this decision caused the president to move it back to its original date two years later. In 1941, Thanksgiving was finally sanctioned by Congress as a legal holiday, on the fourth Thursday in November.

Benjamin Franklin favored the turkey as our country's national bird. "It is a noble bird," he argued. Perhaps it is, but I'm glad he didn't win that argument. Can you imagine eating roast eagle on Thanksgiving?

Better Watch Out, Here It Comes

December 2007

Here it comes again—Christmas is right around the corner. Yes, the Christmas shopping season is upon us, and has been upon us for weeks already.

I am not a good shopper; my wife, God bless her, does it all, but since she doesn't drive, I usually have to go along. For the most part I follow her around and participate very little, except when we go to a book store. Book stores are fun, and, in my opinion, books make great gifts, but like everything else, book stores have changed a lot over the years. It wasn't so long ago that book stores were dusty old places run by little old grey-haired men sitting at a rolltop desk who could tell you exactly where to find any book in the place.

Now, like everything else, they have gone high-tech. They are supermarkets for books, with aisles and aisles of books carefully categorized. I haven't seen any shopping carts yet, but just wait.

It is also very popular with the modern book stores to have a lunch counter. Many years ago, I was in a little book store in New Haven, and there was a coffee bar/restaurant in it. Eat a little, read a little—I liked the idea back then, and the big book store chains must have too. Almost all of them sell food as well as books, which is okay with me. That's one thing they got right.

One of the most fascinating things about book stores is the number of cookbooks that are available. It seems like over a quarter of the shelves are filled with cooking volumes, and right next to the cookbooks, a quarter of the store's shelves are filled with diet books. Seems to me there is some sort of a message lurking there.

Another popular genre is the self-help books. Simply by reading one of these books, you can make bushels of money in real estate, write the great American novel, gain a whole new personality, clear up pimples, and visit the Argosy Casino on ten dollars a day. All those self-help books are very interesting, and probably grist for another column . . .

This holiday season, visit a book store and give someone a book for Christmas.

WHAT'S HAPPENIN'

January 2008

With the start of a new year, I thought it might be interesting to tell you about what has been going on with the Society.

As always, we have been busy. The upstairs room is starting to look pretty good. There is a furnace and air conditioner up there, the walls and ceilings have been repaired and painted, and a new floor has been laid and given a lot of coats of sealer. The new floor looks like a good place to play chess.

Our esteemed leader is looking for an elevator to get us up there easier. Unfortunately, we can't afford an elevator, but Larry has some idea that involves a fork lift, a telephone booth, and eighty feet of quarter-inch cable. I'll wait and see and continue to use the stairs.

Speaking about Larry, how about that Incline float he and his son-in-law built? It is magnificent. It is too bad that it arrived at the parade grounds late and didn't get judged and some of the signs didn't go in the right places, but it was a great float. We would like to use it for other affairs, but it is going to be hard to find somewhere to put it. Does anyone have an old dirigible hanger we could borrow?

By the time you read this, the Organ Crawl will be history. I hope it was a success. Funny thing, I've heard of a piano roll, but I didn't know that an organ could crawl . . .

The Price Hill Historical Society maintains the display at the Covedale Library and has done so since the Library opened. That was ten years ago. We have put in more than 100 displays.

There are lots of other things going on. Just putting out this newsletter every month is a tremendous job and a job well done by the staff and the volunteer folders every month.

Keeping the place running and warm, most of the time, is quite a job also. Those volunteers are to be applauded too. A lot of hard work is done by a mighty few people, but it must be fun, too—because they keep coming back.

If you would consider volunteering, let us know. There is always something to do and we would love to have you . . . Happy New Year!

REFLECTIONS AND THE SILVER SCREEN

February 2008

I would like to reflect on my last column. I mentioned in it that the Organ Crawl was over. I didn't expect the column to be read until after the first of the year. Apparently our newsletter staff are getting more and more efficient and getting it out earlier and earlier every month.

From now on, I will have to be more careful about my timing. I am working on an Independence Day story right now. You never know how far ahead they might get. But I do apologize to the Organ Crawlers. I hope nobody missed it because of my poor timing.

That said, I'd like to talk about the movies. I don't go to the movies very often, but over the holidays, my wife and I took one of our grandchildren, Sam, to see a movie. My first shock was the price. It cost over twenty bucks just to get the three of us in, and this was for a bargain matinee. Then Sam needed some popcorn. Almost five bucks for the smallest bag. Another shock.

But the biggest shock was yet to come. We went into the theater, and they were showing commercials. I was aghast. It's one thing to have to watch commercials on television. They spray their programs out into the air and need some way to make money, but at the movies—give me a break!

I mentally recorded what they were advertising to be sure I didn't inadvertently purchase any of the items that were being promoted. I will boycott them the same way I do with those items advertised in the Sunday newspaper's comic section. Those really irritate me too. They make the comics small enough now, without cluttering them up with ads. And what ever happened to Prince Valiant? (But that's another column.)

They say the movies are better than ever, but the money-grubbing movie houses sure aren't. I remember when you could go to the Overlook for a quarter, even if you were over twelve. More often than not, you got to see two feature pictures, a cartoon, a serial, and even the news of the day. Nary a single commercial. What is the world coming to!

FOLLOW THE BOUNCING BALL

March 2008

No, sorry, this isn't going to be a sing-along. Hopefully, this column will appear in your newsletter that gets delivered on or around March 1, so the subject is what causes March Madness—or basketball—ho, hum.

About this time of the year, groups of poorly dressed young men gather to see who can throw a ball through a ring the most times in a given period. A lot of people find this a very exciting game. In any event, while doing some research for a display at the Covedale Library, I came across a lot of information on the game and decided to pass some of it on.

Most games and sports just grew, like Topsy. They developed from earlier, simpler play and gradually progressed into organized games. These games were improved on, innovations were made, and eventually rules were developed, over time. But basketball was different—it was invented out of whole cloth, as it were, in 1892.

The inventor was Dr. James Naismith, who lived in Springfield, Massachusetts. Naismith was faced with the problem of finding a sport that was suitable for play inside during the Massachusetts winter for the students at the School for Christian Workers. He wanted to create a game of skill for the students instead of one that relied solely on strength. He needed a game that could be played indoors in a relatively small space. He came up with a game that was played with a soccer ball and used two peach baskets as goals. They soon cut the bottoms out of the peach baskets to speed things up.

Amazingly, the ladies took to the game less than a year after it got started. Senda Berenson, Instructor of Physical Culture at Smith College at the time, is responsible for introducing the brand-new game to the distaff side. She changed the rules a little, and of course altered the playing costume. The only body parts that were exposed to the public by lady basketball players were fingers, necks, and heads, even though males were most definitely not invited to watch them play. Nevertheless, proper players wore floor-length dresses on the court. That led to a few broken bones and proper black eyes, because they had a tendency to trip over their hems and go sprawling headfirst on the hardwood court. During the game, the ladies' teams also posted a guard at the doors and windows, lest some man might attempt to peer at them in their dishabille.

You've come a long way, ladies.

THE GREAT INCLINE CLIMB

April 2008

The Price Hill Historical Society recently sponsored a "Scale the Heights Party." Thirty-two members of the Society, plus three members of EPHIA and two from the Price Hill Civic Club, met at Society headquarters on sunny Saturday afternoon not long after that big March snowstorm. A bus was standing by to transport then to the "Foot of the Hill," Glenway Avenue near State. The group planned to climb up the hill, following the route of the old Price Hill Incline.

When they arrived and looked up the hill, twenty-two of them got back on the bus and demanded to be taken to the Crow's Nest. One person just walked down the street to another saloon. The remaining fourteen started to climb. The brambles and brush were thick. The hill was steep. Four of the hikers turned back soon after the trek had begun. A few minutes later, one of the ladies twisted her ankle and another tumbled backwards down the hill. Her husband rushed after her, calling 9-1-1 as he descended. Another man helped the lady with the twisted ankle back to the bottom of the hill. There were only six stalwart climbers left, but they marched on.

It was a warm late winter day, and the sun blazed down unmercifully. None of the climbers had thought to bring water. Soon the hardy climbers were panting and parched. The thorns and thistles had torn their clothes and scratched their skin, so they stopped to rest. When it was time to continue, three of the climbers could not go on. The remaining three reluctantly left them. Their remains have still not been found.

The three remaining hikers plodded on. They pushed and pulled each other up the steep slope. They began to hallucinate. One thought that William Terry had walked along side him, urging him on. Another said that Chief Bold Face had told him to give up and join the Great Spirit, and the third said that Doris Day had sung "Que Sera, Sera" to him.

They finally reached the first street that crossed the path of the old incline, only to find four police cars with lights flashing. They were arrested for trespassing and taken to District 3. Thus ended one of the Society's less successful events.

If all goes well, this column will appear in the April issue of the newsletter. You will, hopefully, be reading it around the first of the month. Be sure to keep that in mind before asking me who the three lost victims were.

LOOKING FOR AN HONEST MAN

May 2008

Do you remember Diogenes? He was that old Greek guy who wandered around with a lamp, looking for an honest man. Even back then, I suppose that was a frustrating job, but just imagine if he were wandering around today in Washington, DC, Our Nation's Capital, looking for that honest man in one particular group of people:

- Twenty-nine of the people in that group have been accused of spousal abuse.
- Seven have been arrested for fraud.
- Nineteen have been accused of writing bad checks.
- One hundred and seventeen have directly or indirectly bankrupted at least two businesses.
- Three have done time for assault.
- Seventy-one cannot get a credit card due to bad credit.
- Fourteen have been arrested on drug-related charges.
- Eight have been arrested for shoplifting.
- Twenty-one are currently defendants in lawsuits.
- Eighty-four have been arrested for drunk driving in the last year.

Poor old Diogenes, trying to find one honest man among the 535 members of the United States Congress. That is the same group that cranks out hundreds of new laws each year designed to keep the rest of us in line.

Editor's Note: This column contains the opinions of the author and does not necessarily reflect those of the Price Hill Historical Society, its officers, members, or anyone else that might disagree with it. But if you disagree with it, well, have you read a newspaper or watched the evening news lately??

SUMMERTIME . . .

June 2008

And the living is easy, fish are jumpin', blah, blah, blah.

Summertime is still my favorite time of the year. I always look forward to the opening of the pool at Philipps.

Although I no longer swim a dozen or so laps, and I can no longer throw myself, twisting and spinning, off the high board (which has been removed for insurance purposes), I still enjoy basking in the sun, soaking up the rays. I no longer worry about the cancers it might cause. If they ain't got me by now, I doubt if they will.

I have spent a lot of my life submerged in water, so much, in fact, that some parts of my body are permanently pruney, so I don't even go in the water very often.

I still enjoy watching the young babes, in their skimpier and skimpier bathing suits. Unfortunately, they seem to get younger and younger every year and those skimpy swim suits are more often diapers.

I still enjoy the couple of weeks we spend at the beach every year. There is nothing more relaxing than sitting on a hot beach drinking a cold bottle of beer.

Sadly, I no longer drink beer, but I still enjoy watching the dolphins and the pelicans diving for fish, even the gulls, fighting each other for crumbs but now it is the abundance of fresh seafood that is available there that attracts me more than the ocean.

I fly a kite once in awhile. I keep experimenting with smaller and smaller ones these days. Not like it used to be, when my kids and I would fill up the sky with a whole flotilla of them.

We used to catch crabs at the beach, lots of them. We caught them by the dozens, cooked them and ate them. They couldn't have been fresher or tastier. Now when I want crabs I drive up to Austin's fish market. They are almost as fresh and almost as good, but some how it's not the same.

Alas, the bird of time has but a little way to fly, and lo, the bird is on the wing. (Apologies to Omar.)

Take Two and Call Me in the Morning!

July 2008

From articles I have written in the past, you have probably noticed that I find television commercials for prescription drugs very offensive. The drug companies probably now spend more on advertising than the automobile companies, more even than the breweries.

Where do you think the money for those ads is coming from? Those commercials are paid for with the money that you and I put out when we buy those expensive prescriptions. That makes us prime contributors to the drug companies advertising budgets, which they then spend to annoy us . . .

My complaints obviously have not been heard, or at least, nobody has paid any attention to them. There are now more of these ads than ever on television.

So, I thought I would write my own commercial. Picture this:

> *Music comes up (instrumental rendition of "Sunny Side of the Street"). Open on a bright blue sky full of fluffy white clouds. Fade in a rainbow. The word "GENERIC" appears, in letters made of gold, on the rainbow. The whole scene fades into a doctor's office set. I am sitting behind a desk, wearing a white smock with half glasses perched on my nose. My face is in profile. I slowly turn my head to face the camera and speak, with a very serious expression on my face.*

DOCTOR: Generics . . . Generics are not for everyone, but just like those expensive, nationally advertised drugs, they can cause itching, vomiting, and dizziness, seldom resulting in fainting. You may experience bleeding from the hands and feet. This usually occurs only in religious zealots. Swelling of the ears, nose, and third toe of the left foot may occur. Do not continue use if you are very rich or have recently received a substantial inheritance. *(Pause)* Always talk to your physician before taking any new drugs.

> *(Music comes up.) Rainbow appears over scene. The word "GENERIC," still in gold, flashes off and on. (Loud music.) And fade out.*

Editor's Note: This article is in no way meant to offer medical advice. The opinions expressed are those of the author and are not to be considered rational.

THE FOURTH REVISITED

August 2008

I was a little surprised this year when I woke up on Independence Day; the air was filled with pows, whistles, pops, and bangs. The reason I was surprised was because these noises usually start around the middle of June.

This year, because of the quiet prelude, I assumed that people were paying attention to the laws that prohibited fireworks. No way—they just saved them for the actual day.

I don't have any real objections to fireworks, outside of their being illegal. I do wonder why so few people get arrested. You would think that the police could just follow their ears and find all of the pyrotechnic maniacs. I have little interest in causing those little explosions anymore, but when I was a lot younger . . .

My cousin and I would start saving our allowances about the first of May. When it came close to the day, we would go over to a little novelty store on Warsaw and lay in our supplies. We probably spent about ten bucks each and walked away with several boxes full of explosives. We didn't mess with Flower Pots, or Snakes in the Grass, or Roman Candles. We were serious noisemakers.

When the holiday arrived, we would go to my grandfather's farm. It was on Glenway, where God's Bible School, or the Cincinnati Theological University, what ever they call it now, is located. I would climb up on the roof of the carriage house, my cousin would situate himself on the front porch of the house, and we would throw firecrackers at each other. We did it all afternoon. Although there may have been minor injuries, no one was ever seriously hurt. We did this until our supplies were exhausted.

When darkness came, we would walk over and sit on the porch of the big house, light sparklers, and watch the firework display at Mt. Echo Park. A few years of that, and the aging process, have dimmed my interest in fireworks.

I live on a hill in South Price Hill. On the night of the Fourth, I sat on my porch. From dusk to well after midnight, I watched an awe-inspiring display of pyrotechnics. Some of them came from the Western Hills Country Club. But for the most part, they were set off in the backyards of my one-day-a-year criminal neighbors. And the display this Fourth of July I witnessed far surpassed any thing I had seen at Mt. Echo as a kid.

All I could think of was how much money was going up in smoke.

Going Up?

September 2008

You may or may not know that the Price Hill Historical Society is trying to get the funds together to install an elevator. An elevator would certainly make it easier to get to the second floor. But elevators can be a mixed blessing.

Elevators are extremely anti-social places. Surely you have noticed that people never speak on elevators. They simply stand there staring at the number board as if they expect the thing to shoot past their floor without stopping.

The standard rule on elevators is that the departing riders get off before those entering get on, but how many times have you seen some burly fellow try to push on before everyone gets off? And how many times have you been in the back of the elevator and tried to get through the crowd at your floor? Those in front act like you are inconveniencing them and refuse to move.

How often have you run for an elevator as the doors were closing and had someone inside act like he was trying to catch the door, just miss, and shrug and smile at you malignantly as the door closes in your face?

Many people have a great fear of elevators. I call this "Climacroclaustrophobia." That's probably not the proper scientific name, maybe it's "Otisphobia."

The worst part about elevators is that I dream about them. I thought this was peculiar to me, but apparently, a lot of other people do, too. If you are one of us, and dream about going up, it could mean that you feel you are going up in the world or that destiny is in your favor. Should the elevator of your dreams be descending, however, it could mean that you feel your personal power and status are on the decline. If your dream elevator is out of order and not letting you off, your emotions are probably out of control.

My particular nocturnal elevators don't act like any of the aforementioned. In my dreams, there is a three- or four-inch gap between the floor of the elevator and the floor I am standing on. It is with great tribulation that I step across that gap, through which I can see twenty floors down. When I get on my elevator, it goes sideways around in a great arc, sometimes ascending and sometimes spiraling downward. Sometimes my elevator is traveling clockwise, and sometimes withershins.

I can only imagine that this signifies that I have a minor fear of heights, which I have managed to overcome, and that my emotions have their ups and downs in a roundabout way.

"SEVENTH FLOOR! Bogey Men, Ogres, Hallucinations, and Things That Go Bump in the Night!"

Jury Comes from the Latin *Juris* (Which Means Law)

October 2008

A *jury*, according to the dictionary, is "a sworn body of persons convened to render a rational, impartial verdict, officially submitted to them by a court, or to set a penalty or judgment." Sounds impressive, but last month I found out that being called for jury duty is mostly just a tedious way to spend a few days.

In America, the system of trial by jury is unique. No other nation relies so heavily on ordinary citizens to make its most important decisions concerning the law. Citizens of Hamilton County who are registered to vote are randomly selected to perform jury duty. But just because you are selected for jury duty does not mean that you will actually sit on a jury.

I received my summons for jury duty in the mail one day in mid-summer. As old as I am, this was the first time I had been selected. I looked forward to it. I made arrangements to park my car near a bus stop so that I could take the rapid transit to town. (Riding the bus was certainly fodder for another column.)

I arrived at the Court House. My first problem was getting through the metal detectors. I rang the bell. I explained to the attendant that I had a pacemaker, even showed him all the cards I carry that tell me to beware of metal detectors. We went round and round and finally I remembered that I had a roll of quarters in my pocket, for the bus fares. I was finally permitted to enter.

I went up to the Jurors' Room on the fourth floor. There must have been two hundred people milling around. I signed in and then went to sit in a corner. About forty-five minutes later, a man named Fritz showed up on a large-screen TV. He spent about two hours orientating us, telling us how to behave and how to dress. As I looked around the room, I noticed very few of the assembled that met this dress code. When he finished, he said that we should listen for our names to be called.

About 11 o'clock, my name was called. I assembled with the rest of those called. We were told that we could go to lunch, but that we must be back by 1:00 pm. When we got back from lunch, we were told that we could go home. That was the most exciting thing that happened in my first week. I am hoping that the second week will be more eventful. I'll let you know.

John Milton, a civil servant for the Commonwealth of England, was probably thinking about juries when he wrote . . . "They also serve who only stand and wait."

What's a Gazziz?

November 2008

Back in the forties at the soda fountain in Doc West's Drug Store (on Glenway, where Bernen's is today), they served a concoction called a Gazziz. The ingredients were kept a secret, but the drink was very popular amongst the pre-teens of the era. Back in those days, soda fountains were very popular with everybody.

And there were a lot of soda fountains in Price Hill. If you started at the far west side of the Hill, the first one would have been at Philipp's Swimming Pool. Then heading east on Glenway, you would have come to the Sweet Shop, and Doc West's fountain was practically next door.

Prout's Corner had four, maybe five, soda fountains at one time. Graeter's was on the corner of Glenway and Guerley. Joe Loebker owned Miller's Ice Cream on Cleves Pike, across from Rulison, and Dow's, up where Hart's Pharmacy is today, had a big one. A couple of doors down was one of Lindner's ice cream parlors (the forerunners of the UDF chain). Lindemann's was on the corner opposite Graeter's, and I think they had a soda fountain too, but I'm not sure.

Further east on Glenway at Rutledge, there was a drug store with a soda fountain, and across the street, where the streetcars turned around, was Loop's Candy Store. Did they have a soda fountain?

Back in those days, I was just a kid, and the Sunset Theater was about as far as I got, so the whereabouts of soda fountains east of there is a little hazy to me.

I think there was drug store with a soda fountain next to the Glenway Theater. I know there was one at the corner of West Eighth and Elberon, and another one at Mahoney's on Phillips Avenue. It seems to me that there was one next to the Western Plaza. There were a lot more soda fountains in the Price Hill area that I didn't travel.

I think that soda fountains were an important part of Price Hill's past. I would like to put together a history of those hideaways of frosty delights.

But I need your help. Surely some of you remember the soda fountains in Price Hill. Maybe you even have photographs. Write to me at the Historical Society, P.O. Box 7020, Cincinnati, OH 45205-7020. Or you can contact me by e-mail at *phhs@pricehill.org*. I will copy your photos and see that they are returned to you.

J-E-L-L-O!

December 2008

At the dinner table a few nights ago, I was enjoying a dish of Jell-o. Whenever the bananas at our house turn black, my wife chops them up and puts them into some Jell-o. We got to talking about Jell-o and foods we remembered from when we were kids.

Jell-o has been around for a long time. I guess it is as popular as ever. You still see stacks and stacks of it on the grocers' shelves. My kids and grand kids never mention it, though. I wonder if they eat it. I know my grandson in Illinois doesn't. He is a vegetarian.

Vegetarians don't eat Jell-o—it is a little known but true fact that Jell-o is made of horses' (or maybe cows') hooves. I bet you wish I had left that little known fact out of this column.

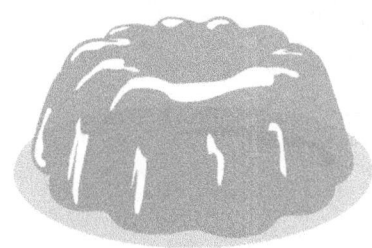

Do people still use Jell-o as a medium to express their secret desire to create great, albeit edible, objects d'art? My mother, aunt, and grandma, all culinary artists, whipped, wiggled, and wobbled various colors and combinations of Jell-o and cast the result into molds, creating shimmering mounds of semi-transparent, quivering goo.

My mother-in-law was the Michelangelo of gelatinous creations. She made Jell-o with little cream cheese worms swimming through it. Another of her favorites was the faux pousse-café, seven different flavors, layered on top of each other. She also had a concoction that involved tossing a can of fruit cocktail into a mixture of Jell-o and whipped cream. She called it Heavenly Hash.

Her sister, on the other hand, was the Stephen King of Jell-o. She used the product for the most ungodly and inedible dishes. If you can imagine it, she was known to have put peas and carrots into Jell-o. One of her favorite things to do was to add a can of tomato paste to a package of Jell-o and pour it into a mold of a fish. The result was a big red blob in the form of a dead fish. It always lay on a bed of lettuce in the center of the table staring at me through its big, opaque, red eyes. How did it taste, you might wonder? I personally have no idea.

With the Christmas season fast approaching, let me offer a suggestion for your festive fare. Mix up a bowl of red Jell-o and one of green (use the lime flavor, the green apple is kinda wimpy). Throw a dab of each on a plate and add whipped cream. Top with two cherries, one red and one green. Your guests will never notice the absence of the traditional mincemeat pie.

"Merry Christmas!"

AND THEY CALL IT FOOTBALL?

January 2009

I don't often write about sports. This column will be an exception.

I just watched a game on television. The Philadelphia Eagles versus the Cincinnati Bengals. It was a game to end all games.

I have never seen two teams try harder to lose a game. With the Bengals it could be expected. They have already lost eight games, but the Eagles—they are not all that good but they have won a few.

Apparently, being good sports, the Eagles decided to allow the Bengals to win, just to bolster their spirits, I suppose. They were determined to lose this ball game.

However, the Bengals resolved that they would not make it easy for them.

Both teams struggled valiantly, doing their best to allow the other to win.

I guess, in a way you could say, that both teams succeeded, for neither team won.

Isn't there a Commissioner of Football? Wouldn't you think that these teams should suffer some kind of a fine?

I am sure there must be some kind of a fine for throwing a game.

Maybe, because both teams were guilty, they evened each other out.

I am sorry, I was so perturbed after watching this game that I had to get it off my chest.

Do you think Toledo might be interested in the Bengals?

⌘ ⌘ ⌘ ⌘ ⌘ ⌘ ⌘

I would like to thank everybody who sent me information on soda fountains that they remembered. I got notes, letters, and e-mails.

I appreciate all of it and I assure you that it will all go into my Soda Fountain File.

Unfortunately, I didn't get any photographs. If anybody has any photos of any of the soda fountains in Price Hill, I would sure like to make copies.

Thanks again, and Happy New Year!

BALLS!

February 2009

Have you ever considered the importance of the ball to modern-day life? Without the ball, life on Earth would be a completely different place. Actually, it would be no place at all, considering that the Earth itself is a ball.

We make a big thing about the invention of the wheel, but if it wasn't for the ball, the wheel would never have been conceived. The wheel, after all, is nothing but an adaptation of the ball.

Without the ball, we would still be getting ink all over our fingers and shirt pockets. The modern ballpoint pen is certainly dependent on the ball. Bicycle wheels, roller skates, roulette wheels, and lazy susans all turn easier because of the ball bearing. Leonardo da Vinci has been credited with the discovery of the principle behind the mechanics of ball bearings. The first patent was awarded to Jules Suriray, a Parisian bicycle mechanic, in 1869.

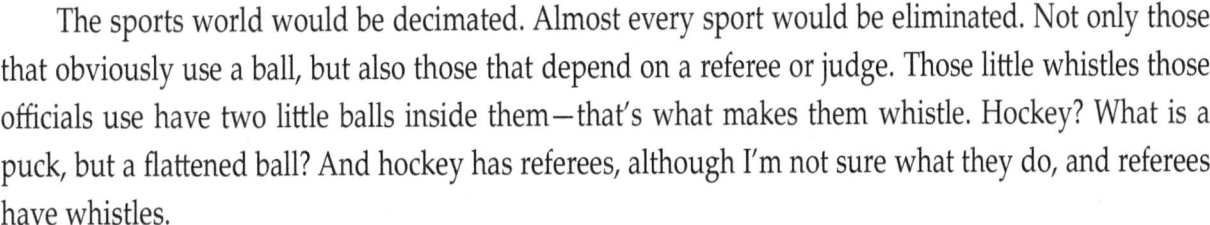

The culinary world would certainly be a lesser place, a place without the meatball. There would be no peas, garbanzo beans, or brussel sprouts. Cranberry sauce would be eliminated from the Thanksgiving feast.

The sports world would be decimated. Almost every sport would be eliminated. Not only those that obviously use a ball, but also those that depend on a referee or judge. Those little whistles those officials use have two little balls inside them—that's what makes them whistle. Hockey? What is a puck, but a flattened ball? And hockey has referees, although I'm not sure what they do, and referees have whistles.

How in the world did the ball get its start? I like to theorize that two little boys living in a rural suburb just out side Paradise Garden found an orange one day. They started tossing it back and forth and soon became very skilled at pitch and toss. Looking for a more challenging game, one of the boys,

Cain, picked up a large boulder. "Go out wide," he yelled as he hurled the rock at his brother. Abel let it slip through his fingers and it hit him in the head. Poor Cain, he was never remembered as the co-inventor of the first ball game, but as the first murderer.

The boys' ill-fated game of toss was duly noted by the elders and the throwing of hard round objects at each other became the most popular way of settling disputes. They soon discovered better and more lethal

(continued on next page)

ways of launching these missiles. Slings, onagers, scorpions, trebuchets, ballistae, springalds, coullards, bricoles, perriers—all are catapults of one type or another.

Some time later the Chinese came up with a concoction called gun powder. By using it as a propellant, they found that their missiles could be launched with greater accuracy and achieve greater distances. Guns, cannons, mortars were invented. The ball as a missile, refined from that first round stone, was becoming far more effective than the misunderstood boy, Cain, could ever have imagined.

The ball, unpretentious, modest, unassuming, simple, is the bright shining star in our world. After all, what is a star but a big ball of gas.

And that's the way the ball bounces.

PITHY MOT

In 1816, a fellow named Thomas Drummond came up with a new and better way to light up a stage. He used a bit of lime heated by a flame and stuck a lens in front of it. These lamps were brighter than anything that had been used previously and were called "Limelights."

Naturally, the actors and actresses on stage tried to get as close as they could to the "Limelights" as they could so the audience would be able to see them better. So, when someone is thrust into public attention, they are said to be in the "Limelight."

OPEN OTHER END . . .

March 2009

Ever since the Tylenol scare a few years ago, a whole new breed of package designers have crawled out of the musty halls of Machiavellian University. These diabolical designers have contrived to produce packaging so tamper-proof that they are almost impossible to open.

I'll give you a good example—child-proof caps. They come with various instructions printed on them: "Push Down, Twist, Pull Up." "Squeeze and Twist." "Lift and Twist." Notice that the word "Twist" is included in all the instructions. That's the part that never works for me. I have found that the easiest way to remove a child-proof cap is to give it to my seven-year-old grandson.

Almost every package containing liquid is doubly protected. The lid is usually protected by a tight-fitting plastic collar that sometimes requires a hammer and chisel to remove. Once you get it off and bandage the numerous nicks and cuts you've suffered, you will find beneath the lid a piece of cardboard or foil cunningly adhered over the opening. It is impossible to get a fingernail under it and pull it off. The best solution is to poke a knife into it and rip. It won't all come off, but you will be able to get to the contents.

The little packets of condiments you find at fast food restaurants are another good example of the malevolent devices of modern packaging. A little packet of catsup has clearly printed on its top, "Tear Here." You can pull and twist and yank and the little packet remains unscathed. Grab the end in your teeth and try to rip it open to no avail. Finally, you grab your plastic fork and stab it. Catsup bursts out, unfortunately, all up and down your sleeve. At this point, I simply rub my french fries on my arm before eating.

The packaging of toys is an art unto itself. They are cunningly encased in a clear plastic shell and are generally wired, glued or, in some cases, bolted to the package. This makes them clearly visible, so as to appeal to the avarice of the child, but also keeps them safe from damage. It takes far longer to remove the toy from the package than the amount of time that the kid will be interested in playing with it. I'd like to meet the designer who thought that was a good idea. Diabolical!

Obama Stimulus Plan to Aid Price Hill

April 2009

Through the combined efforts of several West Side civic and social organizations, funds from President Obama's economic stimulus bill have become available to Price Hill. The plan is to use these funds to create historical monuments honoring our forefathers, the hardy pioneers who, over two centuries ago, climbed up our hill and molded the untamed wilderness into our distinctive suburb.

There will be two memorials, one in East Price Hill and one in West Price Hill. On the east side of our distinctive suburb, the street paving on Warsaw Avenue will be torn out to a depth of six inches. Wooden planks, twelve inches wide and six inches thick, will be laid across the street to simulate the original planked road. The planking will start where Warsaw intersects with Glenway and continue up and around the bend to where the White Castle now stands. The White Castle will be demolished and replaced by a replica of William Terry's original log cabin. The parking area will be torn up and a field of corn will be planted there with a commemorative plaque dedicated to the ancestors. Just south of Grand Avenue, there will be two toll booths, one on either side of the road. These will not be actual working toll booths—the gates will be open at all times so as not to impede traffic.

The memorial in West Price Hill will be located on the north side of Rapid Run, between Lockman and Overlook Avenues. All the existing houses along there will be demolished, the land will be leveled, and an authentic pioneer village, the Village of Warsaw, will be constructed. There will be informational plaques at various locations, visitors will be welcome, and walking tours will be available. A shuttle bus will run regularly from the memorial to and from the CVS parking lot.

A secondary project in this area will be the acquisition of the apartment building at the corner of Rapid Run and Nebraska. It will be torn down and the lot will be leveled; then, the debris from the Warsaw Village Project will be dumped there and covered with earth to simulate the Indian mound that once stood there. Whether or not the replica mound will be included in the walking tour has not yet been decided.

A third memorial was suggested by the folks in Covedale. They requested that Cleves Pike be covered in gravel and horse droppings from Glenway Avenue to Neeb Road, to commemorate the old Cleves Warsaw Pike. This suggestion was denied as being impractical.

It looks like this stimulus thing is going to make some big changes on our hill. And remember, you heard it here, and you heard it on April 1st.

A History Lesson

May 2009

I t was December 8, 1628. It was a Friday. Avery Bensonhaven, the president of New World Tours, was seated in front of the desk of Pinkus Frothingmouth, CEO of the Brighton Boat Building Company.

"We got problems, Pinky—big problems—with our 'One-way Pilgrims' program. Buddy, we are lacking Pilgrims, and that ain't good, pal. Not good at all."

"What's the problem, Benny?"

"You remember that bunch we sent over on the Mayflower? Well, besides getting the natives riled up, stealing their corn and digging up their mounds, they got all the other Pilgrims what come later all ticked off."

"Ticked off? Whadda they ticked off about?"

"Seems like them original Pilgrims are going around saying that they come over on the Mayflower and that makes them better than anybody else, 'cause they were there first. They don't never say anything about that bunch of idiots in Virginia who got there about thirteen years before them, or that crazy Italian fellow, or them horn-headed Vikings way back when.

"It's putting a bad taste in the mouths of all them folks that come later. And it is killing business. Folks just ain't booking anymore—it's killing me.

"That last boat I sent over only had three paying passengers and they weren't even Pilgrims. They was a tinker, a tailor, and a candle-maker, and the boat had to deadhead back."

"That's bad, yeah, but what can we do, Benny?"

"I got an idea . . . a real humdinger. You know that new boat you're building? Name her the Mayflower 2, only spell it Too. That way, everybody in that new, England place can say they come over on the Mayflower, too."

Frothingmouth stared out at the docks as he pondered Bensonhaven's proposal. "Benny, I don't care what we name the boat, but what about the original one? We can't have two Mayflower's running around."

"You busted up the old one a couple of years ago for the old lumber and scrap iron. It's long gone," laughed Avery.

"And those people in Virginia? They certainly can't say that they came over on the Mayflower," mused Pinkus.

"Don't worry about them, Pinky—they're a flighty bunch. They'll probably just wander off someday."

MEMORIES

June 2009

The Price Hill Historical Society is nineteen years old this month. It got started in 1990. A lot of water has gone under the bridge in those nineteen years, at least a lot went under my particular bridge. Back in 1990, I could still twist and flip off the diving boards at Philipps. Alas, no more—old divers never die, they just lose their spring.

Nineteen years, on top of the sixty I had already put in, can cause dramatic changes. Everything that works hurts, and what doesn't hurt doesn't work. You feel like the morning after, and you haven't been anywhere. Your knees buckle and your belt won't. Your back goes out more than you do. You look forward to a dull evening. You finally know all the answers, but you can't even remember the questions. I think the forgetfulness is the worst thing.

A few nights ago, my wife and I were sitting in the living room. I got up from my chair, and Gini asked, "Where are you going?" I replied, "To the kitchen." She asked if I would get her a bowl of ice cream. "Sure," I said. She then asked if I should write it down, so that I would remember what I was going to get. I said, "No, I can remember."

"Well," she called, "I also would like some strawberries on top. You had better write that down because I know you'll forget it." "I can remember, you want a bowl of ice cream with strawberries." Then she added, "And I want whipped cream. I know you'll forget that, so you'd better write it down." I was getting a little irritated and said, "I don't need to write it down, I can remember!"

After about 20 minutes, I walked out of the kitchen and handed her a plate of bacon and eggs. She stared at the plate for a moment, then said, "You forgot my toast."

I know, that's a sad old joke, but it illustrates how our memories fail as time goes by.

Many tell me that these are the Golden Years. If these are your Golden Years, you must have had a very unexciting youth.

Golden Years or not, I would like to extend to all my best wishes and a Happy . . . Ah, uhm, I think it starts with an A. Happy . . . A. A, Ah, An . . . Anniversary.

That's it, Happy Anniversary to us.

Other Books From Edgecliff Press

Drawing Pete
Right, Angels!
I Thought Pigs Could Fly!
Americans Revisited, Vol. 1
Sucking it up: American Soldiers in 2008
Cincinnati's Findlay Market - A Photographic Journey, Past & Present
Managing Nonprofit (& for Profit) Organizations:
Tips, Tools and Tactics
Pre-Victorian Homes

And From Edgecliff Kids

Alena and the Favorite Thing
Hobo Finds a Home
Cliffie's Life Lessons

**Look for more titles from
Price Hill Historical Society
and Edgecliff Press, LLC. soon!**

www.ingramcontent.com/pod-product-compliance
Lightning Source LLC
Chambersburg PA
CBHW080833250626
47160CB00008B/2919